SHADOW OF THE DRAGON

Shadow of the Dragon

SHERRY GARLAND

HARCOURT BRACE & COMPANY

San Diego   New York   London

Library of Congress Cataloging-in-Publication Data
Garland, Sherry.
Shadow of the dragon/Sherry Garland.—1st ed.
p.   cm.
Summary: High school sophomore Danny Vo tries
to resolve the conflict between the values
of his Vietnamese refugee family
and his new American way of life.
ISBN 0-15-273530-5   ISBN 0-15-273532-1 (pbk.)
[1. Vietnamese Americans—Fiction. 2. Refugees—Fiction.
3. Family life—Fiction. 4. Gangs—Fiction. 5. Interracial
dating—Fiction.] I. Title.
PZ7.G18415Sh   1993
[Fic]—dc20   93-17258

Designed by Lisa Peters
Printed in Hong Kong
First edition
A B C D E

For Karen Grove and Erin DeWitt,

with many thanks

Prologue

Danny Vo saw the oak tree and shivered as if a winter wind had blown through the open car window. He and a new friend had stopped for the red light in front of the old Linda Vista Apartments where Danny once lived. The buildings were crumbly and sad looking, even worse than when all of the occupants were Vietnamese refugee families like Danny's. Now another wave of refugees from another war lived there.

Danny would never have turned down this street himself, but he wasn't driving, so he had no choice. He couldn't tell his friend not to go down the street because of a creepy oak tree, a tree that neighborhood kids swore was haunted. So Danny sat in the passenger seat, trying not to look but unable to turn away from the dull green leaves and twisted trunk.

The oak tree had suffered over the past three years. One of its limbs was broken, probably by rowdy kids. And a hunk of bark had been skinned off, probably from the bumper of some drunk's pickup after he'd missed his turnoff from the main street. It used to happen all the time when Danny lived there.

But the metal tray was still there, girdling the trunk about four feet off the ground. An old woman, stooped from too many years of working in the rice paddies of Vietnam, had just placed fresh mangoes and flowers and a bowl of rice on the tray. A whiff of sandalwood drifted through the car window from the stick of incense she had just lit.

Danny's American friend was curious. He wanted to know what the old woman was doing and what the metal tray meant. Danny told him that somebody the old woman loved had been killed under that tree and that she was making sure the departed spirit had plenty to eat in the afterlife. What Danny didn't tell his friend was that the shrine was also meant to appease the restless spirit lingering nearby to keep it from harming the living.

When Danny's friend asked who got killed and how, Danny just shrugged and said "some teenager." He pretended he didn't know much about it. But he did know. The old woman in the baggy black pants and gray high-collared shirt was his grandmother, and Danny had known the dead teenager very well. It seemed like a lifetime ago, in another time and place, not a mere three years.

It was difficult to think about those days when his world circled around a blond-haired girl named Tiffany Marie and when he learned about love and about sacrifice.

As the red light changed, Danny let his breath out with a long sigh of relief. But the chill didn't go away for the rest of the day.

Chapter One

Danny Vo jammed his hands into the pockets of his blue jeans, hoping no one from school would see him grocery shopping with his mother. But there was little chance of that. It was a late Saturday morning and only two weeks before what Americans called Chinese New Year, and what the Vietnamese called Tet. All the Asian shops clustered on Houston's Bellaire Boulevard bustled with customers. Up and down the narrow aisles of Di-Ho Market, women and children, and an occasional man, bumped elbows as they bought food for the upcoming stream of New Year's parties.

Old women in baggy black pants lingered over the fruit and flower stands selecting ripe persimmons, small round winter melons, or fresh-cut gladiolus for the family ancestral altars. Children laughed and dashed around tables spilling over with neatly packaged plastic boxes of candied ginger, dried mandarin orange peel with licorice root, sweetened lotus seeds, fried melon seeds, and sugar-coated strips of coconut dyed pink, yellow, and green.

Danny's mother paused over the stacks of *banh-chung* and *banh-giay,* New Year's cakes wrapped in banana leaves and neatly tied in square or round bundles. With determination, she turned her shopping cart away. She insisted on saving money by making those kinds of foods herself, even though it took a lot of work and time.

Danny glanced over the top of his short mother's head. He didn't want to be here. He had a hundred other things to do. There was going to Radio Shack with Calvin Pickney to buy some electronic parts for their joint science project. There was talking to Mr. Tilson about getting a job in his grocery store a block from Danny's apartment. And then there was driving past Tiffany Marie Schultz's house in hope of seeing her outside. There was always that.

Danny saw two Vietnamese girls from his high school. Quickly he turned and stooped down, pretending to examine the long, golden-green stalks of sugarcane under the vegetable bins. After the girls had passed by, he picked up a stalk and carried it like a kung fu staff toward his mother's cart.

The only good thing about this shopping trip had been driving his father's car. Danny needed all the practice he could get before taking his driver's road test when he turned sixteen. Only he already was sixteen, according to his Vietnamese birthday. It was because of a mix-up on the legal immigration papers his parents signed when they arrived in America ten years ago that Danny was always counted as half a year younger than he really was. If his parents, fresh from Vietnam and unable to speak English, had better understood the INS officer, they would have explained that Vo Van Duong, who later changed his named to Danny, was born in the year of the Dragon. It was the luckiest symbol in the Vietnamese zodiac and almost guaranteed the child a life of success, if he applied his talents.

Danny's parents had been confused by the American way of counting birthdays. It was the first of a very long series of misunderstandings that his parents fell prey to. But the American officials had been too busy processing dozens of refugees that day to worry about a few errors on birth records here and there.

Sometimes Danny hated his parents' screw-up. He would have had his permanent driver's license right now, if it hadn't been for their ignorance. Although he only had his beginner's permit, he sometimes drove alone anyway, even though he wasn't supposed to. He kept telling himself that he wasn't *really* breaking the law, since he *really* was sixteen. And as soon as he got his license and a car, he could get a job. Although his parents wanted their oldest son to concentrate on school, even they had to admit that another wage earner in the family would bring them one step closer to their biggest dream—buying a house and someday owning their own business.

Danny followed his mother, rolling the sugarcane between his fingers. She steered her cart down an aisle spilling over with dozens of different kinds of rice noodles. The starchy smell of rice blended with the sharp, almost nauseating odor of dried cuttlefish and black mushrooms from the next aisle over. He watched her loading up neatly tied bundles of needle-thin *bun* noodles, wondering if his mother was the only one in the market who was buying food for an occasion other than New Year's. It seemed unlikely.

"Má, you've already got a ton of noodles at the apartment. How many people are coming to Sang Le's homecoming party, anyway?"

"I want to be prepared," she replied in Vietnamese that was slightly tinged with an American accent. "You never know who might show up. Your father and Uncle Dao have been telling everyone that your cousin Sang Le is finally getting out of the refugee camp. Everyone wants to welcome him to America. I must have enough food. We can't let people think we are cheap." She paused and pointed to a fifty-pound sack of rice. "Pick that up for me."

Danny stuck the sugarcane into her cart, then hoisted the rice bag to his shoulder. He decided to carry it that way. At least now he wouldn't look so wimpy to the two teenage girls watching him from behind a table littered with fruit baskets wrapped in red cellophane. Danny had seen the girls at his high school before and thought they must be sisters. They wore the same old-fashioned skirts and blouses and hairstyles— long, straight, with thick, blunt-cut bangs. They didn't wear makeup and had flat chests. They definitely were not his type. They reminded him too much of photos he had seen of boat people or girls living in communist Vietnam today.

The sisters fit in fine here among the rice paper and mangoes and banana leaves, but in school Danny had heard Americans making fun of them behind their backs. The same thing had happened to him when he first entered the American schools. He hated to admit it now, but back then he pretended to be Chinese just so kids and even adults wouldn't ask him about the war, or about being a Vietcong, or living in a grass hut, or accuse him of having dogmeat in his lunch box. He got tired of telling them that he wasn't even born until after the war and that he had been too young to remember much about Vietnam. He learned very fast to dress and eat and talk like the American kids. Danny swore ten years ago that no one would ever have a reason to make fun of him again. And nobody could call him "uncool" now.

Danny wondered how long the sisters had been in Houston. They probably didn't even realize they were out of step with the other girls at school, but he wasn't going to be the one to tell them.

The shopping cart reached an impasse near the butcher's counter where several children hovered near glass tanks filled with live fish and tubs of live crabs and snails. The kids were jabbing sticks into the crab bed and squealing each time a pair of pincers snapped at them.

When Danny's mother reached an aisle with rows of colored tins of tea, she picked up one marked "fragrant jasmine."

"Maybe I should have some nice tea for your cousin. I wonder if he prefers jasmine or lotus fragrance?"

"Má, Sang Le's been in a Hong Kong refugee camp for the past two years. And before that he was a prisoner in a communist re-education compound. I think anything you serve will look like a feast to him. He's probably not very choosy."

Danny leaned against the shelf. He had not seen his cousin for ten years, when he was six and Sang Le was eight. Back then in Vietnam, his cousin had seemed as tall and straight as a bamboo shoot. But now Danny could not remember his cousin's face or the sound of his voice. Like everything else about Vietnam, he had stored away the memory of his cousin on a back shelf in his brain.

"Don't we need to be getting home pretty soon if I'm going to drive to the airport to get Sang Le?" Danny impatiently shifted the rice bag to the other shoulder.

The short woman glanced up at Danny with

her large eyes. A layer of makeup could not completely hide the dark circles under them. Danny knew she had stayed up most of the night cooking fancy foods and preparing the apartment for the homecoming party. And all that after working eight hours at the seamstress factory where she sewed curtains, and then four more hours at her part-time job as a waitress on the late shift at an American restaurant. A wave of affection swept over Danny. He squeezed her shoulder with his free arm.

"You need to go home and rest before the guests start arriving," he said gently.

Her full lips pouted a moment, then she waved a delicate hand tipped with long pink nails.

"Okay, okay," she said with a thick accent. "You get drinks. I get one more thing. You alway hurry, hurry." She shook her head.

With his free hand, Danny pushed the cart to the soft drink section and piled in some twelve-packs of Sprite, Coke, and a carton of canned soybean drinks for the little kids. The sack of rice slung over his shoulder was getting heavier by the minute, but he couldn't put it down. It was a matter of honor. The two teenage girls had inched their way closer to him, stealing glances, whispering and giggling. When his eyes met the liquid dark eyes of the taller, prettier girl, he gave a crooked grin, trying not to grimace from the pain throbbing in his shoulder. The girl had a beautiful face, but she still wasn't his type.

"Hurry up, Má," Danny pleaded as he rejoined his mother by pots of miniature mandarin orange trees and buckets of gladiolus and chrysanthemums. She picked up an artificial tree covered with delicate yellow silk flowers dotted with dark gold centers.

"I think I'll get this *hoa mai* tree for your grandmother. In Vietnam she always bought a fresh tree branch every Tet."

"She won't like it," Danny said. "She'll say it's not alive; it's not from Vietnam; it's too cheap looking. You know how Bà is."

Danny's mother bought the *hoa mai* anyway, paying for it and all the groceries in cash. She looked at her wallet, empty except for a couple of twenty-dollar bills. She didn't say anything, but Danny knew she was wondering how they would make their money stretch through the New Year's season. They still had to buy presents for the children and have at least one more party. And now there was the added burden of his cousin Sang Le coming to live with them.

Danny tried to push the thoughts from his mind as he helped his mother carry groceries to the car. He plopped the sack of rice into the trunk of his Dad's old Toyota and rubbed his shoulder. He noticed that the two teenage girls had come out behind him, snacking on what looked like a bag of dried, candied plums. Danny didn't know why he kept looking at them. They were really too old-fashioned looking for his taste. They probably didn't even speak English or go out on dates. He'd never seen them with American friends at school. Their mother probably had taught them to never look a boy in the eye, to keep their thoughts to themselves, and to never display affection or emotion in public, for that was a sure sign of rudeness or even worse, sexual aggression. At least that was what his grandmother was always trying to pound into the heads of his younger sisters.

Danny imagined the two girls were trying to work up the courage to speak to him, probably just to say "hello." Why couldn't they just walk up, wave, and say, "Hi, Danny, how ya doing?" like Tiffany always did? Why all the mystery?

After a few minutes the Toyota's trunk was full of grocery bags. Danny had been lucky to find a parking spot so close to the store. Di-Ho shopping center was crowded every Saturday, but around the Lunar New Year, cars packed the lots. Danny had tried explaining to his American friends how important the New Year was to Vietnamese and Chinese people; that it was more important than Christmas. But he didn't think they really understood any more than he could understand why some of them got so excited about football games.

As he closed the trunk, Danny glanced over his shoulder to see if the girls were still watching. He thought he might wave, or smile, or throw them a kiss, just for the heck of it. He didn't think he was all that handsome, just sort of average in most ways. He wore his hair in a popular style and tried to dress in good clothes. He kept in good shape by running almost every day, playing tennis every chance he got, and lifting weights occasionally with Calvin. Girls were always telling him he had gorgeous eyes and a cute smile, so he guessed he was all right. Besides, girls like those two standing on the sidewalk were probably desperate for attention from any guy.

When Danny looked over the top of the car at the girls one more time, his eyebrows shot up. The girls were huddled together, their backs pressed against the brick wall near the old Chinese movie theater. Four Asian boys were leaning close, talking to them. The boys looked like older teenagers, though one might have been in his twenties. All four boys wore blue jeans and black leather jackets with golden silk emblems stitched on the backs—the expensive kind of jackets that Danny wished he could afford to buy.

Danny couldn't imagine the shy girls carrying on a conversation with those guys. The boys must have just stepped out of Ho's *bida* hall a few paces away. *Bida* was the Vietnamese word for billiards.

Two of the boys puffed on cigarettes. The smallest wore his straight hair pulled back in a short ponytail. He blew a stream of smoke into the face of the taller girl. She must have expressed her disgust, because suddenly the guy grabbed her arm and jerked her from the wall.

Danny froze.

"What's wrong? Why you take so long?" his mother asked from the passenger seat. "Hurry up, hurry up! That's what you tell me."

"Just a second, Má."

Danny gently closed the door and cautiously worked his way through the parked cars toward the sidewalk. He was sure now that the girls didn't know the four boys. Their eyes were wide with fear and the tall girl was crying. Danny stopped five feet away and cleared his throat.

"So, there you are," he said in Vietnamese

as he put his hands on his hips. "Come on, sisters. Mother is waiting." He stepped closer, grabbed each girl's arm, and pulled them from the wall. He smiled at the four boys and shrugged. "Sorry. Hope my sisters weren't bothering you. Hey, nice jackets." He noticed that the emblem on the back of each jacket was a golden cobra with blood-red eyes, its head raised off the ground, full-blown and poised to strike.

The oldest boy, the short one with the ponytail, glared at Danny with sharp black eyes. Danny wondered if he was high on something. He'd never seen eyes so intense. The guy might have been in his early twenties, it was hard to tell. His chiseled features should have been handsome—the high cheekbones, the neat, small mustache, and thick, finely arched eyebrows— but his lips turned down at the corners in hard anger, ruining the face.

"You better teach your sisters some manners," he hissed. He dropped his cigarette on the sidewalk and ground it with the toe of his expensive boot. His foot was tiny, almost feminine. With Danny towering over the fragile man, he looked as if he could be pushed over by a puff of air or the touch of a feather. But the look in his eyes made Danny think twice before making a move.

As the ponytailed man turned, light flashed off his gold neck chain and bracelet. Danny didn't even want to think about where the money for them came from. He just wanted to get away as fast as possible.

"You sisters ugly, man," a boy with chubby cheeks said. He reminded Danny of a greedy chipmunk, and his flattop and a tiny gold earring in one ear only served to emphasize his roundness. The boy stuck his plump fingers into the shorter girl's hair. "They gonna be old maids."

All the guys laughed. Danny felt the short girl's arm trembling in his hand. He was glad they weren't really his sisters. Words like that should have meant a fight, but why take the risk for a couple of strangers?

Danny forced a wary grin and shrugged.

"It's the curse of our family—ugly women. You should see their mother."

The chubby boy stopped laughing and drew in a sharp breath. All eyes turned to the small one with the ponytail. Everyone held his breath. Danny felt a bead of sweat roll down his back in spite of the cool weather.

Suddenly the leader relaxed and grinned. His face looked almost human, except for the black eyes.

"You okay," he said in poor English. "Cobra

let you go this time." He hissed like a snake, then shifted his weight to his back leg and arched his hands the way old men did in the kung fu movies Danny's father often rented. Danny suddenly remembered the cobra he had once seen at the zoo. Even though it had been behind a glass cage, the sight of it had made chill bumps creep along his arms. That same chill rippled through his body now.

Cobra moved his hand so fast that all Danny saw was a flash of silver, and then he heard a soft snap. He had not even known that Cobra was holding an opened butterfly knife all the while he had been talking. Danny nodded to Cobra, then pushed the girls toward his father's Toyota.

As Danny shoved the girls into the backseat and started the car with a roar, his mother's mouth flew open.

"Good morning, ma'am," the girls said in polite Vietnamese.

"Uh . . . Má, these are some friends of mine from school. I told them I would give them a lift to the other end of the shopping center. If it's okay with you."

Danny's mother nodded, but she didn't take her eyes off the four boys in black jackets who were swaggering across the parking lot.

The Toyota shot out of the lot, drove about a block, then slowed in front of the curb at the end of the long shopping center.

"Get out of here and run like crazy," Danny whispered to the tall girl as she scrambled out of the backseat.

The two girls broke into a run and didn't stop until they stood in front of Kim Phuong Restaurant. The taller girl hesitated at the door a few seconds, staring at Danny, before her sister pulled her inside.

Danny took several deep breaths to calm his nerves as he leaned back into the driver's seat.

"Why were you talking to those boys?" his mother asked.

"It was nothing, Má."

"Who were those girls?"

"I told you, just some friends from school. They needed a ride. It was nothing."

"Those boys are very bad. Stay away from them. They're no good. They belong to a *toan du dang*. They're like pieces of trash in the gutter. We used to see them in Da Nang during the war." Her lips turned down and for a moment Danny thought she was going to spit. He'd never seen her so upset about him talking to some boys. She usually didn't mind who his friends were, as long as he stayed out of trouble.

"Never, never go with them," she said in a shaky voice.

Danny noticed that she was trembling, so he switched the heater on.

"I didn't know those guys, Má. I wasn't being friendly with them or anything like that, honest." He tried to place a hand on her arm. She pushed it away and didn't seem to even know that he had spoken.

"I know those kinds of boys," she muttered, more to herself than to her son. "Just like Da Nang. They're no good."

Suddenly she grabbed Danny's arm and squeezed with all her might.

"Promise me you will never get mixed up with those bad boys!" she almost screamed.

Danny swallowed hard and tried to concentrate on his driving. He had already made an illegal turn and just now almost ran a red light and had to slam on the brakes. He didn't understand why his mother was acting so crazy all of a sudden, but it was affecting his nerves.

As Danny waited for the light to change, a silver convertible with its top up crept out of the shopping center parking lot. The driver of the car saw Danny and pulled up beside the Toyota. A thin smile crept across Cobra's lips and his black eyes glinted. The chubby boy mouthed the words "Where are your ugly sisters?" then cackled.

Danny glanced at his mother. She was looking the other way, out of the passenger window, lost in her own thoughts.

Danny watched the convertible screech away as the light turned green. He accelerated slowly, letting them get a long head start.

"Don't worry about me, Má," he said softly. "I'm going to keep as far away from that gang as I can."

Chapter Two

The smell of lemon grass, tangy *nuoc cham* sauce, and smoke from a charcoal grill greeted Danny's nose as he carried the heavy sack of rice up the outside stairs leading to their second-floor apartment. Out on the spacious concrete landing that also served as a patio, his uncle Dao squatted on his heels beside the grill, fanning smoke away from his watery eyes. Marinated strips of pork woven on bamboo skewers lay on a platter covered with plastic wrap. Even though it was the first day of February, the weather was mild, with only a few clouds gathering on the horizon. A pleasant breeze lifted Uncle Dao's straight, thick hair, revealing beads of perspiration.

Danny paused at the threshold lined with pairs of shoes in all sizes. Even before he turned the handle, he heard arguing.

"Bà and Kim are at it again," he said to his mother as she stopped behind him.

"Alway fighting," she muttered. "You have to settle it."

Danny pushed the door open for his mother, then carried the rice bag to the pantry and dropped it with a thud. A woman they called Aunt, even though she was not kin to them, stood over the sink grating carrots for the pot of *nuoc cham* sauce on the stove. Uncle Dao's wife, Lien, sat at the table flipping through the pages of a fashion magazine. Not long ago she changed her name to Linda, for the same reason that Danny changed his when he turned twelve. He got tired of his teachers and other students pronouncing his name "doong" because they didn't realize that the letter "d" is pronounced like a "y" by southern Vietnamese. Even Kim did not use her real name, Hien, because she was taunted and called "henny-hen" or "chicken breath."

As always, Aunt Lien looked like a fashion model in her perfectly coordinated clothes, with her long manicured nails and permed hair that curled softly to her shoulders.

"Hi, Danny," she said in English, "you look cool today."

Before Danny could reply, two children burst into the kitchen. The oldest, a spindly girl of nine, grabbed a can of soybean drink from the carton before Danny put it on top of the refrigerator.

"*Anh-hai,* Bà and Kim are fighting again." She called him by the traditional name for the firstborn son. *Anh-hai* really meant "second son." But calling the firstborn the second-born helped deceive the evil spirits who preferred to steal away the oldest son, the most honored of positions among siblings. It was one of those things that was too rooted in thousands of years of mystery for Danny to explain to his American friends, so he always told them that *anh-hai* meant big brother.

"What's it about this time, Lan?" Danny asked as he glanced over the swinging half-doors that separated the kitchen from the living area.

The little girl shrugged.

"I'm not sure. They're talking too fast." She began taking groceries from the sacks, then spied the sugarcane and grinned. She cut off a piece about two inches long, peeled back the golden-green skin, then sank her teeth, minus the front two, into it.

"I think it's Kim's short skirt," Danny's younger brother, Thuy, said as he popped the top on a Sprite and sipped it warm from the can.

Danny nodded. He figured the fight would be about something like that. It always was. Kim was the most headstrong child in the family. And even though their father couldn't hide the fact that she was his favorite, he still swore that she was responsible for putting every gray hair on his head.

"Has Cha come home yet?" Danny asked, glancing toward the living room again, hoping to see his father. "Did he get the day off like he wanted?"

The boy nodded. "Yes, but he's busy working on Má's car with Uncle Nghia."

Danny sighed. He should have remembered that. The reason he had driven his mother to the market was because her car was broken and she couldn't handle the stick shift on the old Toyota.

"Go in there and settle the fight," Danny's mother urged as she swished the children out of her way. "You know Kim never listens to me anymore. You are the oldest son. You must discipline your sister when your father isn't here."

Danny expelled air from his lungs slowly. For the hundredth time he cursed this Vietnamese custom. Calvin Pickney was the oldest son, too, but he never lifted a finger to settle family disputes. It was Calvin's sister Lashandra who ordered all the kids around. If Calvin so much as opened his mouth in protest, she would slap him across the room.

Sometimes Danny liked the power of ordering his siblings around, but he hated settling fights, especially when Bà was involved. Danny took a deep breath before pushing the swinging doors open and stepping into the living room. The arguing suddenly stopped and two pairs of equally black, angry eyes glared at him.

The old woman, dressed in baggy black silk pants and a dull gray high-collared blouse, came only to the shoulder of her granddaughter. Not a single gray hair was out of place in the tight knot twisted on top of her tiny head. She must have been a prune in another life, Danny thought as he stared at the wrinkles around her eyes and skinny neck.

Suddenly both females started talking to Danny at the same time, one speaking Vietnamese, the other English.

"Hold it, hold it! One at a time, please. Bà, you first," he said in a soft, even tone and bowed slightly.

"Grandson, tell your sister she cannot wear those disgraceful clothes," the woman said in old-fashioned Vietnamese, the kind not corrupted by a single word of English and difficult for Danny to follow. "I am ashamed to be seen with her.

She looks like something that stands on the streets of Saigon outside a bar." The old woman shook a gnarled finger tipped with long, yellowed nails.

As his grandmother continued explaining why decent girls did not dress like Kim, Danny eyed his sister. Of course Bà was right. Kim's black stretch skirt was so short it would be impossible for her to do anything except stand up all day. Her eyelids were blackened, like a raccoon's, and her lips looked like something out of a vampire movie. She'd been messing with her hair again. A few months back she had started snipping off fractions of her long black hair every night, hoping Bà wouldn't notice the gradual change. Their mother was understanding and liked short hair, but everyone knew the old woman would throw a fit if Kim cut it all at once.

Then one night Kim had come home from a friend's house. The girls had given each other permanents. What a mess. Curls so tight she looked like a poodle. Now it looked as if Kim had experimented again. This time her hair had a bright orange-blond streak through one side and it stuck up on top like a crane's nest.

Danny tried not to laugh. Kim had been okay as a kid, just a little headstrong. When she turned twelve, though, she went crazy, buying movie and hairdo magazines, wanting to spend more time at her girlfriends' houses than her own home, and talking on the phone to boys night and day. Danny's mother complained about her daughter, but working two jobs left too little time to supervise Kim.

Danny waited until Bà had finished, then folded his arms.

"All right, Kimmy, what's your story?" He fingered the price tag dangling from her newly purchased purple leather jacket that twinkled with silver studs. Beneath it a black mesh blouse showed.

"*Anh-hai,* all the girls at school dress like this."

"Ha!" Danny rolled his eyes.

"Oh, how do you know? You're not in junior high anymore. Times have changed in the past two years."

"Oh yeah, right. I guess you think I'm in another time warp. As if I never see any thirteen-year-old girls. My school is right across the street from yours, remember? I see you skinny-legged girls walking down the road every day."

"Well, what's wrong with my clothes? They cost me all the money I had saved up. Aunt Linda says I look cool."

"Ha!" Bà interrupted impatiently. "My daughter-in-law is a hair's breadth from being a Saigon tea-girl. Why do you want to look like that when your cousin Sang Le comes home? Nice girls do not dress like that in Vietnam. What will he think about us, letting you look like a tramp? And your relatives from all over town and from Port Arthur and Galveston will be here. I will have to go into the courtyard and hide my face against the brick wall."

Danny wanted to smile, but he didn't dare. Kim put her hands on her hips and whirled around.

"Anh-hai," she whined, "I told her already, I'm not going to be here for the party. I promised my friends I would go to the movies this evening. Má told me I could go."

"When did she tell you that?"

"I asked her a week ago."

"That was before she knew exactly what day cousin Sang Le's plane would be arriving. Don't you think you should be here to meet him?"

"But I already told my friends. They're expecting me!"

Bà made a clucking noise with her tongue. "Shh . . . you are too selfish. You are *chi-hai,* the oldest daughter. It is your duty to be in the kitchen helping your mother and aunts or watching over the little children."

"I cleaned my room and the living room and the bathroom," Kim protested. "I washed the clothes and put the pork on the bamboo sticks. Lan gets to go to the airport with you, Danny. You're always going out with your friends. Why can't I?"

"Duong is a boy," Bà replied before Danny could speak. "It is too dangerous for decent young girls to go out. Some awful old man may get you."

"She's right about that, Kim," Danny said. "Somebody might beat you up for that jacket. Of course, he'd have to be color-blind."

"That's not fair! I always have to stay home and do house chores. Americans don't have to do that."

"Shh, granddaughter. You should be thankful that you have a home and a family. Your cousin lost his home and his country, just like me; just like your parents and your uncle. Don't you realize, child, you can lose everything else, but if you have family, you will survive. You *must* be here to show your cousin Sang Le your love and support. Your family comes before friends."

"I don't care about Sang Le."

Bà threw her hands into the air. "Ah! Such disrespect. That's what comes from your mother working night and day. She is never home to teach you how to act. You only listen to your wild friends."

Danny knew Bà's words were falling on deaf ears. It would do no good to try logic on Kim, either. She had a stubborn streak a mile wide.

"Danny . . . please." Kim turned to her brother with pleading eyes. "I worked a long time to save money for these clothes." When he hesitated, she put her hands on her hips, then blurted out, "Forget you, I'm going to go ask Cha."

"That's right," Bà screeched. "Go to your father. He spoils you like an emperor's daughter, but he is not here this time."

"Then I'll go ask Má." Kim spun on her bare feet. Apparently her savings hadn't been enough to buy the knee-high boots she needed to match the leather jacket.

"Good! Let Má make the decision!" Danny shouted at her back, then stomped off toward his room. The less he was involved in family disputes, the better he liked it.

As Danny reached his room, he heard another round of arguing, this time coming from the kitchen.

"Anh-hai!" his mother called out.

"Yes, Má," Danny said with a sigh of resignation and returned to the living room door.

"*You* must settle this dispute," she said, casting an angry glance toward her daughter. "Now Kim says she does not want to stay for the homecoming party. She will not listen to me anymore. And your father is too busy and too tired to be bothered with such trivial problems. *You* are the oldest son and *you* are responsible for the manners and welfare of your younger siblings."

"But . . . what do *you* think about Kim's clothes?"

"I think they look terrible, but she says all American girls wear them. I don't know if she is lying or not. You know about American clothes better than I do. Please, Duong, I'm too busy with cooking and getting ready for your cousin's party to argue with Kim." Her dark, tired eyes blinked as she sighed and pushed a lock of hair away from her sweaty brow. Suddenly Danny felt guilty for bothering her.

"Please hurry," she added. "You will have to go to the airport very soon. Thuy, go get your father and tell him it's almost time for the airport," she said to her youngest son, then returned to the kitchen without another glance at Danny.

Danny sighed. "Okay, okay," he muttered and pointed to the sofa. "Sit down, Kim. If you can manage."

Kim started to protest, but he pointed again

and narrowed his eyes. Kim sat sideways, jerking at her skirt and putting her hands over her bare thighs.

Danny took his grandmother by the arm and gently led her to the overstuffed chair across from Kim. Her frail body didn't make a dent in it.

"Bà," he said softly as he dropped to his knees in front of her and took her withered hand in his. He struggled to pull the correct Vietnamese words from his brain, trying to speak accurately and clearly so the old woman would understand. "You are right to protest the way Kim is dressed. It isn't the best way for a thirteen-year-old girl to be seen."

Kim huffed, crossed her arms, and slammed back against the couch. Her red-black lips pouted like a puffer fish.

"But," Danny continued, "Kim worked hard to earn money so she could buy some of her own clothes. We told her when she took that baby-sitting job that most of the money would be hers." He did not know the Vietnamese word for baby-sitting, so he had to interject that phrase in English.

The old woman grunted and crossed her arms, too.

Danny bowed his head, stared at a brown stain on the worn carpet, then rose to his full height. What did it matter what his decision was? he thought. Nobody would be satisfied.

"Okay, I've made my decision. Kim, you can't wear that skirt. Change into a longer skirt or pants. You can keep the jacket and blouse. But comb your hair down and take off that ridiculous lipstick and eye junk. You can go to the movies tomorrow, but for now you have to stay home in case Má needs you in the kitchen."

"That's a stupid decision. You're not being fair, Danny. I already told my friends—"

Danny held up his hand. "That's it. Another word and the jacket and blouse go back, too. Now, go call your friends and explain why you can't go today. The movie will still be there tomorrow."

Kim glared through dark, glistening eyes before jumping to her feet and running into her bedroom. The force from the slammed door knocked the wall clock, the one made of polished cypress wood and shaped like Vietnam, to the floor. It slid between the goldfish aquarium and the family altar that Bà had so painstakingly decorated that morning.

Bà rose slowly. She muttered under her breath as she shuffled toward the kitchen, but she stopped at the swinging door. Over her shoulder she called out, "You're not strict enough. Your decision stinks."

Danny replaced the clock, then walked down the hall, pausing at Kim's room. The loud rock music couldn't completely drown out her sobs. He tapped lightly.

"Kimmy, don't take it so hard. Look, I'm doing you a favor by stopping you from wearing those clothes in public. You look awful, you know. Maybe you can go with us to the airport. How's that?"

"Shut up!" Kim screeched. A loud thud shook the door. It was probably the Vietnamese-English dictionary she kept on her dresser. He tried to turn the doorknob, but it was locked. It was his two sisters' good fortune to have the only bedroom in the apartment with a lock, apparently installed by the last renters.

"Okay, have it your way," he muttered as he opened his bedroom door.

Danny stopped. Plastic Ninja Turtles, comic books, and a handful of miniature cars covered the floor and the two new bunk beds his parents had bought for Thuy and Sang Le. On Danny's single bed lay a sleeping baby and a toddler. Danny stepped back into the hall and called Lan and Thuy.

Without a word the little girl picked up the

baby and woke the toddler. She took them into the living room. Thuy quickly picked the toys up off the beds and the floor, saying, "Sorry, Danny," as he hurried out.

Danny closed the door, then stretched out on his bed and sighed. He didn't mind the little ones; they never gave him much trouble. It was easy to settle their fights because he was bigger and never wrong in their young eyes. Kim was another story; so was Bà.

Sometimes Danny wished the old woman didn't live with them. She was about the nosiest person he'd ever seen. He had to hide things from her because she respected no one's privacy. She always had an opinion about everything she saw, even if she had no idea what it was used for. She hated almost everything American—food, cars, music, clothes. But she did like television and VCRs. Her favorite pastime was watching the Vietnamese TV station or the twenty-volume sets of Vietnamese movies that Uncle Dao brought home from his Asian video store downtown. She preferred the weepy love tragedies with ghosts and kung fu. Of course, she always found something to complain about in the movies and would never admit she liked anything Aunt Lien picked out.

None of the grandmothers of Danny's

American friends lived with them. Calvin Pickney's grandmother didn't. Danny had met Calvin's grandmother once. She was nice, quiet, and sweet. She gave Cal ten bucks for no reason at all. It hadn't been his birthday or Christmas or New Year. Bà wouldn't part with a nickel if her skinny life depended on it. She kept her money squirreled away in a tin can buried someplace in the backyard. And she wouldn't tell anyone where it was, not even Danny's father, her third oldest son, the one who had found a place for her on the boat when the family fled from the communists in Vietnam.

Danny leaned over and opened the drawer of a nightstand next to his bed. It was covered with nicks and scratches—a two-dollar "treasure" from a garage sale. His grandmother had bought it, as excited and tickled as a little kid. She couldn't stop bragging about how much money she'd saved him on bedroom furniture. And then she'd gone into a long speech about how wasteful Americans were, always throwing away perfectly good clothes, furniture, and food.

Danny hated the nightstand, but he couldn't say anything to Bà's face, for that would be disrespectful. And the oldest son had to set the example for the others to follow. That was why Bà blamed him for Kim's behavior. In her eyes, if he had been a perfect example, Kim never would have gone wrong.

Danny removed a science magazine from the nightstand drawer, then flipped to page one hundred, where a Polaroid snapshot was fastened with a paper clip. He rolled onto his back and sighed. A smile touched his lips as he held up the photo and let the light fall onto a pretty, petite, blond-haired girl. She was holding a garden hose in one hand and a soapy sponge in the other while standing next to a 1967 red Ford Mustang. Her cutoff blue jean shorts and tight-fitting stretchy knit top showed off her trim figure at its best.

"Your grandmother doesn't live with you, Tiffany Marie," he whispered. He kissed the glossy picture. "And I bet you never argue with her or with your mother, either. Why should you? You wear great clothes, not stupid weird stuff like Kim. You probably do your homework, help with the dishes, watch TV, listen to the radio, and go to sleep. Bet your house is quiet and peaceful and spotless, like you."

Danny sighed, closed his eyes, and pressed the photo to his cheek. He remembered the way Tiffany had looked yesterday, standing beside her open locker. She always had a big, friendly grin for him. She smelled great, too. Not that stinky, cheap perfume that choked you—the stuff that Kim and her friends wore. Tiffany's perfume was soft, subtle, and lighthearted, just like her. It made him think of a field of wildflowers on a warm spring day. The kind of day he imagined he would spend with Tiffany, if he could ever get a date with her.

Danny's lips curled up slightly as he dreamed how wonderful it would be to walk through a flowery meadow with Tiffany Marie Schultz at his side, holding her hand, smelling her sweet perfume, and touching her silky blond hair. He'd never been in a field of wildflowers, but it sounded good the way Tiffany had described it in the essay she read in front of English class last year. She had been describing her grandparents' farm somewhere in the middle of the state near a place with a name like Pleasantville, or Heavenville. Maybe it had been Paradise.

"*Mmm,* Paradise," Danny said out loud. "That's what it would be like with Tiffany Marie. Paradise."

A loud thump rattled the bedroom door. Danny's eyes flew open and he quickly hid the snapshot. The noise sounded again, followed by children's laughter and yelling and sharp, dog yelps. Danny leaped up and jerked the door open. Three kids pretending to be dogs rolled onto his feet.

"Time to leave for the airport," said a small, compactly built man standing at the end of the hall, drying his hands. Danny nodded to his father, then ran a comb through his thick black hair before hurrying down the hall. He paused at Kim's door.

"We're leaving now, Miss Kimmy," he shouted. "Have you changed clothes? Do you want to go to the airport with us?"

He heard nothing inside the room except muffled radio music. Danny pounded harder with his fists.

"Kim! If you're not out in one minute, we're leaving you behind. This is my last offer."

He waited, got no reply, then shrugged. As he crossed the living room, he had to step over two sleeping babies on a pallet and walk through a circle of children playing a board game. The kitchen buzzed with lively conversation from three men sitting at the table sipping beer and tearing off strips of dried cuttlefish to eat. Four women chattered near the sink as they washed fresh mint leaves, chopped cucumbers, and stuffed and rolled *cha gio,* small Vietnamese meat rolls.

In the corner, Danny noticed the yellow potted tree that his mother had bought at the market.

"How did Bà like the *hoa mai*?" he asked

his mother as he leaned over a huge aluminum pot of boiling broth.

"Hmmph!" she snorted. "What do you think? It's in the corner, not in the living room."

Danny grinned but didn't say "I told you so."

"We'll be back from the airport in about three hours," he said as he placed a soft kiss on her warm cheek.

"Duong is so tall and strong," one of the women said. "He looks like a wrestler."

Danny flushed. At school he wasn't even considered average in height. His friend Calvin was already five-foot-ten. He hurried outside and opened the driver's door. This would be the longest distance he had ever driven since getting his beginner's permit. He was a little nervous but proud that his father trusted him. Two other cars were already filled with family friends, waiting for him. He had been chosen to lead the way, since he could read the overhead directional signs near the airport, a confusing process if you didn't understand English.

Danny glanced over his shoulder as he fastened his seatbelt. He saw his Uncle Dao, Bà, and Lan in the backseat. His father sat in the front.

"I don't know how we're going to squeeze

one more person in the car," Danny complained as he started the motor. "Where's cousin Sang Le going to sit?"

"There's always room for another relative," Bà snapped, breaking her icy silence. "We never turn away a member of the family. Especially when he needs help so much."

"I didn't mean it that way, Bà. All I meant was maybe Lan should stay home so Sang Le won't feel so crowded in the car."

"She can sit on my lap," Uncle Dao offered and lifted the little girl onto his knees. "Your cousin Sang Le is used to lots of people around him. This car is going to be like the emperor's yacht to him." Uncle Dao tickled the girl's ribs, making her double over with giggles.

"I feel like I'm in a parade," Danny mumbled as the two other cars got in line behind him. He was surprised when his grandmother spoke. She must have ears like a fox, he thought.

"We have to welcome Sang Le with lots of relatives and friends so he will feel at home," Bà said. "We are the closest family he has, now that his mother and father are dead." The old voice cracked with emotion. "He is the only son of my only daughter. He is my blood and he is your blood. You must make him feel welcome."

"I know, I know," Danny muttered. He

decided to give up trying to communicate with his grandmother. She seemed to misinterpret everything he said, even when he was agreeing with her. Suddenly Danny felt a sharp slap on the back of his head from Bà's hand. He winced and gripped the steering wheel to keep from cursing.

"Show some respect," she screeched. "Remember, Sang Le saved your life once."

Danny heard the old woman clear her throat and knew what was coming next. She was going to tell *the* story again.

"Bà, please . . . not again," he protested.

"It was the first day of Tet, in 1982," she began in a low, crackling voice, ignoring Danny's plea. "You were only six years old. We had gotten permission from the communist pigs to return to Hue, the beautiful city of my birth, to tend the graves of our ancestors so their spirits would have a safe, joyful passage to earth. Oh, what a relief to be away from those crowded, miserable streets of Da Nang, where I was forced to flee in 1968 after bombs destroyed my home in Hue.

"Your mother had sewn you and baby Kim each an *ao dai* from cloth of an old dress. No one ever knew they weren't brand-new, and my relatives in Hue thought we were much better off than we were. Your cousin Sang Le and his mother, my precious daughter, Nga, were there for the family reunion at my brother's house. I had not seen Nga for so long. Ah, how skinny and pale she looked. And little Sang Le was all sickly and weighing the same as you, Duong, though he was eight years old and taller."

"Bà, please, everyone already knows the story." Danny felt the heat creeping to his neck and cheeks. He wanted to roll the window down for fresh air, but he knew the old woman would complain.

"The air of Hue was wonderfully clear that day," she continued. "We could smell flowers and fruit from the marketplace and wild reeds from the River of Perfumes. We strolled along the bridges over the lotus moats around the imperial palace. How I had missed that grand old place. My eyes wept when I saw how it had been ruined by bombs and rockets and bullets. Water buffalo and chickens prowled around the very courtyard where I had watched the last emperor, Bao Dai, climb on top of an elephant for a parade. Ah, it was pitiful, I tell you, pitiful.

"I was weeping openly and Nga and your mother were trying to comfort me. We didn't even notice that you and Sang Le had climbed down to the moats. Of course, it was too early in the year for the lotus to be in bloom, but the seed pods were rattling in the wind and you were squealing with delight. You tried to pick one and fell into the water. Little Sang Le, with only his skinny arms, reached in and pulled you out, though it made him fall in, too. He almost drowned, and he developed a terrible lung infection. He almost died. Now, that is sacrifice, to save the life of another with no regard for your own safety. You children today know nothing of sacrifice. You think only of yourselves. You have it too easy in America. But, of course, that day was the beginning of all their troubles." She sighed, and in the rearview mirror Danny saw her dark eyes shimmering. "But I don't want to talk about it today. Today we will be happy that Sang Le is coming to us."

Danny felt the tension slide from his body, and he slumped back against the seat and slackened his grip on the steering wheel. He was glad she chose not to finish the story, for it was not a pleasant ending. Sang Le's mother, Nga, refused to come to America when Danny's family found a boat to freedom two days later. She would not leave her sick child behind to die. And in order to get medicine for her son, she signed some papers that the communists put in front of her—papers that indicated her husband was part of a conspiracy during the war. He had been in a re-education camp, which was really nothing more than a prison, since 1975. A year after she signed the papers, her husband died. The officers reporting the news said he committed suicide because of her betrayal. She shrieked and raved and struck out at them, calling them murderers. When one of the soldiers knocked her to the floor, Sang Le came to her rescue. He was arrested and put in a re-education camp in Long Binh. Sang Le was nine years old. Nga blamed herself for everything and committed suicide not long after that. Without a husband and child, she saw no reason to live.

Danny felt the sickening taste of guilt, as he always did when hearing that story. He knew he owed his life to his cousin, and if he had not fallen into the lotus moat maybe Aunt Nga would still be alive and happy in America. Maybe she would have remarried and Sang Le would be a freshman honor student at an exclusive university.

Danny sighed. He was truly glad that Sang Le had finally been released from the Long Binh re-education camp and then had escaped to China. Danny knew he should be glad his cousin was free at last from the squalid refugee camp in Hong Kong where he had lived the past two years. He *was* happy for Sang Le. But as Danny entered the freeway, he couldn't stop thinking about how his life would change with another teenage boy in the apartment. Other refugees who had come from Hong Kong told horror stories about the living conditions. Privacy probably meant nothing to Sang Le. Sharing a room with Danny and Thuy surely wouldn't bother Sang Le at all. Everyone seemed so concerned about Sang Le's comfort and happiness. But what about his?

When Danny's family first came to Houston, they had lived in a government housing project. Danny could hardly remember anything about it except living by a bayou with snakes and frogs. Then they lived in a two-bedroom apartment across from an elementary school. It was convenient but too crowded.

The day the family moved into a three-bedroom apartment everyone was hysterically happy. At last Danny had a little more privacy and space. But now that same apartment seemed like a shoe box, and all his parents talked about was buying a house, and later buying a business. It was their number one dream, the dream that made his mother hold down two jobs and his father put up with insults and low wages at the assembly plant where he worked. The family would work together for their common good, just as two years ago his parents and Bà had loaned most of their savings to Uncle Dao to buy a video store downtown. Dao's in-laws had also loaned him money. As soon as Uncle Dao's business was running smoothly and making a profit, he in turn would repay the money to Danny's parents and give them a loan to buy a business of their own. And when they became successful they in turn would help someone who had helped them. It was an endless chain of borrowing and loaning money among relatives and friends. Banks were rarely needed.

Danny didn't blame his parents for wanting a house and their own business, but the goal seemed unrealistic now that Sang Le was coming to live with them. They had spent half of their savings to get him to America. Just another sacrifice in the name of family unity. Danny hoped it was worth it.

The first drops of rain began falling as Danny changed lanes and eased the Toyota onto Interstate 45. He had been so absorbed in his own thoughts that he had not even noticed the clouds moving in. He would have been even more nervous about driving if he had known he would have to deal with slick streets and dirty windshields.

Danny heard his grandmother whisper something to Lan. The little girl giggled.

"Rain brings good luck," Lan sang out. "Bà says that dragons bring the rain to earth and the clouds are their shadows. Bà says cousin Sang Le is going to have good luck in America because he is arriving in the shadow of a lucky dragon. Is that right, Danny?" Lan leaned over the front seat. Her breath smelled like sugarcane.

Danny had believed those fairy tales when he was small, too. How many times had Bà told him how all Vietnamese were descendants of a dragon-lord and a fairy princess; how they must always act honorable and brave and be willing to sacrifice like their dragon ancestor. And always Bà told him that rain was the gift of the gods, the giver of life across her homeland, from the steamy deltas ripe with rice to the lush mountain jungles. Rain was to be appreciated and respected.

Danny's American friends always said the rain was gloomy and sad. It spoiled their holidays and weekend fun. Maybe dragons only brought rain and good luck in Vietnam. As Danny looked at the darkening sky and the thick, rolling black clouds, he fought off a shiver.

"I hope Bà is right, Lan," he replied. "It's about time Sang Le had some good luck."

Chapter Three

Cold rain pelted the side of the car inching down the highway. Danny clenched the steering wheel and strained to see through the fogged-up windshield. He could barely see the taillights of the cars ahead of him or the headlights of the cars that had been following him for the past hour and a half. He wasn't even sure they were the cars of his family's friends.

"We're going to be late," Bà's voice crackled from the backseat. "You should not have left the driving to a boy for such an important mission. The airplane has already landed. What will poor Sang Le think when no one is there to meet him?"

"Mother," Danny's father said in a calm, even voice, "Sang Le has been waiting all his life to come to America. Fifteen minutes more will not matter to him. Duong is doing the best job he can. I know the windshield wipers are stuck on low speed. I've meant to get Dao to work on them, but he has enough problems of his own."

"And what is that supposed to mean?" Uncle Dao challenged.

"You know what it means," Bà blurted out before Danny's father could reply. "That wife of yours is causing too many problems. Better you make her stay home and take care of her babies."

"There's nothing wrong with Lien wanting to go to cosmetology school. She can start her own business one day. You know she hates working in my store downtown. She says it is too boring and too dangerous."

"Ha! Better she works with you. It looks bad for a wife to not help her husband. I worked in the rice fields for twenty years beside your father before he was called to war. Never would I think of leaving my children alone. What is beauty college for? Beauty should come from the heart, not from paint on your face and lips."

Danny groaned. The last thing he needed was another argument between his uncle and his grandmother. Uncle Dao and Aunt Lien had not even visited their apartment for over two weeks because of the last fight. Danny heard the old woman grunt and saw her black eyes and pouting lips in the rearview mirror.

He tried to close out her high-pitched voice and concentrate on his father's encouraging words about his driving. But still Danny felt the pressure of knowing that everyone in the car and those following were depending on him to get them to the airport on time. Maybe he shouldn't have volunteered so eagerly, even though it was good practice.

Danny's heart pounded as two eighteen-wheelers cradled the small Toyota between them, spraying the windshield with a sticky coat of dirty water. Beads of sweat rolled down his temples and back, but he didn't reach for the heater. Every time he had tried to turn it down, the old woman complained about being cold. Whenever he tried to switch lanes, unable to see very well through the foggy, dirty windows, she would take little gasps and mutter under her breath.

When Danny missed the airport exit, Bà began to wail and they lost ten more minutes circling back. Danny had imagined that traffic near the airport would be light, but he soon found himself in a long line of cars inching their way past each red light. By the time they reached the airport it was almost two o'clock.

"Forty-five minutes late," Uncle Dao said

with a wink and clamped his hand down on Danny's shoulder. "Not so bad. After all, we're on 'Vietnamese time.'"

Danny felt his face turning red as his father and uncle laughed lightly. He knew they weren't being critical. Being on time was never important to older Vietnamese. To them, arriving early only made them appear too eager. Still, Danny felt like a failure, especially in his grandmother's eyes.

Inside the main lobby, Danny was the only one in their party who could read the flight schedule monitor. He had hoped his cousin's plane would be delayed because of the rain, but it had landed on time, delivered in the mist and rain as if in the arms of a protective dragon.

They hurried to the terminal, only to find the waiting area empty. Danny couldn't imagine where Sang Le would have the nerve to go. He didn't speak English and surely wouldn't feel brave enough to wander around.

"Maybe he met a Vietnamese-American on the plane and followed him to the coffee shop," Danny suggested. "Why don't we page him?"

"He no understand English so much," Danny's father said in choppy English. "Better we look for him."

They divided up into small search parties and

agreed to meet back at the lobby in twenty minutes. Bà and Lan stayed in the waiting room. Danny headed toward the parking garage. Maybe someone had told his cousin to go there to wait for their car.

As Danny stepped through the glass doors, a blast of cool, damp air hit his face. He turned up the collar of his denim jacket and shoved his hands into the pockets. Even though the rain had stopped, the weather was wet and miserable. A porter in a navy blue uniform nodded to Danny.

"Excuse me, sir. Have you seen a Vietnamese boy come this way in the past half hour, looking kind of lost?"

The man squinted one eye and rubbed his prickly chin, then nodded. "Was he real skinny? Wearing last year's throwaways?"

"Probably."

"Yeah, I saw him walking up the exit ramp a few minutes ago. I yelled at him to watch out for cars coming down. Told him he might get run over, but he kept on going like he was deaf."

"Thanks," Danny said and began to run. His sneakers tapped on the concrete at a steady pace even though going uphill was killing his calves. He was glad he was in good shape from running nearly every day on the high school track. He had been on the freshman tennis team but had to quit because it was interfering with his grades too much. Quitting the team had been painful at the time, just another of the many "sacrifices" that Bà insisted would help build his honor. "It's easy to sacrifice when you are young, to build a better future," she had said as he lay sprawled on his bed that day, almost in tears. "Study hard now, don't play too much. Your parents work hard and sacrifice so you can have a good education. Later, when you reap the rewards of a good job, you will repay them. Everyone must work together."

Squealing tires and the rumble of a motor echoed down the ramp. Danny pressed his body against the wall and felt a blast of warm air and exhaust fumes as a car zoomed by. He wondered if his cousin would have the sense to get out of the way of exiting cars. Did they even have cars in Vietnam? Danny wasn't sure, and he couldn't shake the image of his cousin lying on the concrete, flattened by a pickup.

Danny paused briefly at each level to shout Sang Le's name. The orange level, the blue level, the yellow, the green—finally Danny reached the rooftop, gulping for air. His dark eyes darted from car to car until he saw something in the far corner near the railing.

Danny let out a long, ragged breath, squared his shoulders, then trotted toward the slender teenager leaning over the rail.

"*Chao anh,* Sang Le," Danny greeted his cousin.

The boy's thin shoulders jerked, and he whirled around, his legs braced for a fight. His dark eyes had the look of a cornered wild animal.

"I'm your cousin, Vo Van Duong," Danny said in Vietnamese. He held out his hand. "Welcome to America."

Slowly the teenager's rigid body relaxed and a soft smile crept across the dark face shaded by a blue-and-orange Astros baseball cap. It was the only new piece of clothing on the boy's body. His shirt, yellowed from years of washings and frayed at the sleeves, hung loosely over a pair of khaki-colored pants rolled up to just below his knees. His skinny legs stuck out like toothpicks and ended in a pair of cheap plastic sandals. Danny stood a good five inches taller than his older cousin and weighed at least thirty pounds more. He couldn't believe this stranger was the boy who had seemed so tall when they were children.

The word "refugee" seemed to drip from Sang Le's rain-streaked face. Danny wondered if his own parents had looked so pitiful and frightened when they arrived in America ten years ago.

"Hello, honored cousin Vo Van Duong," Sang Le said in his native tongue as he bowed from the waist. "It is a pleasure to see you. I wish you and your family much health and happiness . . ." He broke into the long, formal greeting that the old-fashioned Vietnamese give to each other, the greeting that Bà made her grandchildren use with older people.

"What are you doing up here on the roof?" Danny asked.

Sang Le's face looked blank. "Please say that again," Sang Le said in Vietnamese. "Sorry, but I did not understand. Are you speaking English?"

Danny laughed. "Well, I *thought* I was speaking Vietnamese. I said, What are you doing up here?" He spoke more slowly and pointed to the rooftop.

Sang Le smiled. "You have a very strong American accent. You are very hard to understand."

Danny shrugged. "What do you expect? I *am* an American. And you're not very easy to understand, either. You speak that old-fashioned Vietnamese just like Bà."

"Bà? Is she with you here at the airport?"

Danny nodded.

"Good. I will be so happy to see her again. I was only eight when she left Vietnam. I missed her so much over the years."

Danny tried to keep a straight face. He wasn't going to be the one to disappoint Sang Le. He would just let his cousin find out for himself how much fun Bà could be.

"Are you ready to go back down?" Danny asked Sang Le.

"Just one more minute, cousin. I came up here to see America. I couldn't see from the plane because of the clouds. I stood in the room with chairs but when no one came, I couldn't wait another moment. I had to see what freedom looks like." Sang Le turned back around, his slender fingers clenching the iron rail as he leaned over the roof. His skinny chest swelled with air. "Do you smell the freedom? I have waited so long for this day, the day I am truly free. Ah, it is so beautiful, isn't it?"

Danny stared at the view. On a good day you could probably see a couple of miles, but in the mist and clouds and smog, all Danny saw was pine trees and a few buildings.

"Is that the Empire State Building?" Sang Le asked.

"No. That's a hotel. Come on, everyone's waiting for you."

The trip back down the ramp made Danny's

knees ache. He noticed that Sang Le's spindly legs stretched taut with wiry muscles as they trotted down. His cousin didn't complain or groan and was not out of breath when they reached the bottom and returned to the lobby.

Everyone from the three cars was waiting. The minute Bà saw her grandson, she howled and tears streamed down her cheeks. She clutched him in a death grip, her frail body shaking with sobs. She and Sang Le spoke so fast, Danny could not follow. Then his father and Uncle Dao and some family friends all hugged Sang Le and shook his hand at the same time, each one trying to out-cry the other. Sang Le's eyes were flowing, too, but he remembered to bow and repeat the formal greeting to each adult he met.

At last they piled into the car. Sang Le's only piece of luggage was a battered 1940s-looking straw suitcase that must have been left over from the French occupation. Danny shoved it into the trunk as his cousin settled in the back between Uncle Dao and Bà. Lan moved into the front and curled into her father's lap.

As Danny steered the car back into traffic, he saw Sang Le lean over as if he were fidgeting with something.

"I brought you a present from Vietnam,"

Sang Le said softly to Bà. "I wanted to bring you something of great value, but I had no money. And in the refugee camp we were not allowed to go into the city. But a friend of mine smuggled this out of Vietnam and gave it to me as a going-away present. I hid it inside my rolled-up pants cuff so the airport security men would not see it. I wish I could give you something better . . ." His voice trailed off into a sigh.

Danny heard his grandmother gasp.

"Oh! It is wonderful!" she whispered. "Wonderful! It's the best gift I have received since I've been in America."

The car was stopped at a red light, so Danny glanced over his shoulder. His grandmother held what looked like a dried-up twig in her shriveled fingers.

"What is it?" Lan whispered to Danny. He shrugged.

"It's *hoa mai*," Bà explained in a trembling voice. "It is the New Year's flower of Vietnam. I have not seen one for ten years. Thank you, grandson." She squeezed Sang Le's arm. "Oh, you are so much like your mother. You have her eyes and her kindness. I thought she was gone from me forever, but now I see her living in you, my precious treasure." Her dark eyes glowed as she looped her skinny arm through Sang Le's own slender arm, then slipped her hand into his.

Danny glanced at his father's face. It looked strange and his eyes glistened; so did Uncle Dao's. The air in the car was suddenly heavy with memories. Danny could almost feel the hot, humid air of Vietnam, almost hear the scream of jungle birds, the patter of monsoon rains on thatched roofs. The laughter of children riding a broad-backed water buffalo through flooded rice paddies seemed to echo in the swish and hum of the busy highway.

For an instant, a childhood memory flashed through Danny's mind—an old woman with a smiling face, not quite so wrinkled, sitting under the full moon, telling fairy tales about emperors and dragons to little boys and girls while they sipped hot jasmine tea and ate moon cakes.

Danny blinked once to clear his eyes. It was funny. He hadn't had a pleasant memory about his childhood in Vietnam since his first year in America ten years ago. Now suddenly he remembered that evening of *Tet-trung-thu,* the Mid-Autumn Moon Festival, vividly. He remembered the feel of Bà's silk *ao dai* on his bare legs as he climbed into her lap beside his cousin. He remembered the taste of hot jasmine tea and the smooth, sticky texture of moon cakes and the sweet, delicious fragrance of fading lotus blooms drifting into the courtyard from the river. He remembered the sound of whispering reeds and moaning bamboo and the melancholy notes of a wooden flute as some lonely boatman played a melody from his heart. But most of all, Danny remembered the old woman's soft, melodic voice as she told the tale to the wide-eyed, enthralled children.

"Long, long ago," she began her tale, "there were no people in our land. No huts dotted the hillsides; no farmers walked behind water buffaloes plowing the rice paddies; no emperors sat upon golden thrones; no little children twisted impatiently in their grandmother's lap.

"But there were dragons roaming the earth and they were the wisest, bravest, and most honorable of all creatures. And there were fairies—beautiful, kind, gentle women who looked like humans. One day while searching high atop a misty mountain for a meal of sparrow—a dragon's favorite meat—a handsome young dragon-lord named Lac-Long-Quan encountered a lovely fairy princess named Au-Co, who was gathering willow branches to use as magic wands.

"They fell in love on first glance, and Lac-Long-Quan carried Au-Co away to be his bride. Down the mountainside they flew, riding on a great misty blue cloud that left a river of rain in its shadow. Au-Co's long silk sash and many-colored robe trailed behind them streaking the sky like a rainbow.

"Now, being a dragon, Lac-Long-Quan had to live near water, and being a mighty prince, he preferred to live by the sea. That night, on a bridal bed made of mother-of-pearl (a gift from the Jade Emperor himself), he wrapped his powerful arms around his bride. And their union created one hundred pearly dragon eggs that hatched into one hundred perfect sons.

"As the children learned to crawl and walk and talk, their dragon father grew more irritable every day, for the youngsters got into everything. If he tried to nap under a gnarled banyan tree, the little ones scrambled up his spiked back and under his bearded chin, or swung from his antlers.

"Likewise, Au-Co found the children underfoot all day long. When she tried to gather peony blooms or boil a pot of jasmine tea, always some little boy played hide-and-seek and got tangled in her silken robes, or swung from her sash, or stole her tasseled magic wand and hid it away.

"As the children grew older, the dragon-lord and the fairy princess realized that they could never reconcile their differences. Au-Co was deathly homesick for her misty mountains, but her husband refused to move away from the sea he loved so much. Their affection for each other began to wane until one day they decided they could live together no longer.

"With tears in her eyes, Au-Co said farewell to the dragon-lord and to half of her children. Then she gathered up the remaining fifty and returned to the mountains to live forever.

"Lac-Long-Quan felt a great ripping pain in his heart when she said good-bye, but he could not bear to leave the sea and knew this way was best. He was very grateful for the fifty children who stayed behind with him and settled near the sea. When the children grew up, the oldest son, Hung Vuong, founded his own kingdom and became its first emperor. He was the first of the great eighteen Hung dynasty emperors. The kingdom grew and was filled with happy people. That was our country and those were our ancestors.

"Many, many years later, the Chinese swept down the mountains into our kingdom and enslaved the people. Many brave men and women fought and gave their lives to win their country's freedom. And over the years others came and tried to conquer Vietnam, but always our people were brave because they were the children of the dragon. You must always remember you have the blood of a dragon flowing through your veins."

"But we don't look like dragons," Danny remembered saying in childish confusion, holding his hand in front of his face.

"That is because you also have the blood of a beautiful fairy in your veins. On the outside you look like a human, but on the inside you have the heart and soul of a dragon. Although you will never look like a dragon, sometimes you will be called upon to act like a dragon. You will be called upon to make sacrifices that will rip your heart into ten thousand pieces, but you must be wise and strong and brave. And even though the rest of the world will think you are a mere human, you and I will know that your heart is the heart of a dragon. You must never forget this; you must always remember who you are."

Danny recalled wrapping his small arms around Bà's neck and kissing her face while she laughed lightly. And later that night, while lying on his woven straw mattress next to Sang Le, when the moon was small and silver and sinking over the mountains, he had dreamed he was floating over the earth on a rain cloud, and when he breathed, his breath was misty blue.

Danny wondered if Sang Le remembered

that night and all the others they had shared with their grandmother in what now seemed like another lifetime. He glanced in the rearview mirror and saw his cousin's gaunt face and dark eyes staring back at him.

Danny had hoped that somehow his life would not be changed by the arrival of his cousin, but now he knew that was an impossible dream.

Chapter Four

If Sang Le had been swept up by a flying saucer and dropped on another planet, he could not have shown more curiosity. Everything, no matter how ordinary, caught his attention. He never stopped asking questions and pointing to buildings and cars and highways.

When they arrived at the small apartment, packed with too many people to count, he commented on the luxury of it all. He was overcome with emotion as he opened each welcoming gift—socks, cologne, a watch, thongs, a belt, a baseball cap, some school supplies. No matter how inexpensive the gift, he thanked the giver as if it were made of gold.

Everything mechanical in the apartment fascinated him. He particularly had an affection for flushing the commode. He wanted to disassemble it on the spot to find out how it worked. He would flush and giggle, flush and giggle, then wash his hands again and again at the sink. The electric toaster threw him into convulsions of laughter and, of course, his eyes grew wide as he stared at the television. It wasn't that he had never seen these things in Vietnam, but his mother had been too poor to own any of them, and the refugee camps scarcely could afford such luxuries.

Danny tried to count the people in the apartment but kept losing track of the children, who never sat in one place for more than three minutes at a time. Every bedroom bulged with sleeping babies or children playing games, except for Kim's room—her door remained closed.

When Danny heard rapping at the front door, he sighed. How could another person fit? It was already in defiance of the law of physics. Being the closest to the door, he jerked it open.

He found himself speechless as he stared into the faces of the two teenage girls he had rescued from Cobra at the supermarket earlier that morning. Although he never knew who to expect at a party like this, since the word seemed to spread to every corner of the city, he never imagined *they* would be standing at his front door.

"Chao anh," the pretty one said softly. She held a small present wrapped in leftover Christmas paper with a silver foil bow on top. Danny wondered if his face was as red as hers. Her sister, who was several inches shorter and had a face too harshly chiseled to be pretty, didn't blush. She didn't smile, either.

"Our uncle is coming. He is right behind us," she said in a firm voice, as if that fact would explain why they were on his doorstep.

"Well, uh . . . come on in. It's a welcoming party for my cousin Sang Le. I guess your uncle knows my father, or something like that." He opened the door wider to let them in.

While they slipped off their shoes—the kind he had seen in the Vietnamese shops downtown—a small, stout man with a heavy black mustache stepped to the top of the landing, carrying a bottle of Remy Martin cognac. Before Danny could step aside to let the three of them in, his father rushed forward and bowed to the short man.

"Come in, come in, Mr. Khanh. This is my son, Duong," Danny's father said in rapid Vietnamese. Then he quickly said something about Mr. Khanh working at the plant with him. Maybe he was the foreman. As usual, when his father spoke Vietnamese that fast, Danny always lost a lot of words and only came away with a general idea of what was said. The girls seemed to have no problem at all understanding.

"These are my nieces, Hong and Cuc," Mr. Khanh said. "Their parents are still in Vietnam. The girls have been attending an American high school for six months. Maybe they can help your young nephew with ESL class."

Danny's father nodded and smiled a little too generously. "Duong, show these young ladies to the refreshments," he said, then led Mr. Khanh to the living room, where all the men sat on the floor around a sheet covered with bowls of food and cans of beer. Danny steered the girls toward the kitchen, where the women chattered around the table or hovered near the sink slicing vegetables, boiling shrimp, and replenishing the ice in the men's glasses. The *hoa mai* twig sat in the middle of the table in his grandmother's fanciest vase and seemed to be the focal point of conversation. At least it was the only thing Bà wanted to talk about.

"Má, this is Hong and Cuc. Their uncle works with Cha."

"Oh, what pretty names," Bà said with a nod after the girls had bowed to each woman and repeated the usual greeting of respect. Danny tried not to smile. His grandmother had a strange notion of what names sounded good.

"What do your names mean?" he whispered to the pretty one, Hong.

"You don't know?" the older one, Cuc, asked sharply, speaking her native tongue. "Don't you know Vietnamese?"

"I don't know those old-fashioned names." Suddenly Danny realized he was speaking Vietnamese. It irritated him that Cuc had put him on the defensive. He switched to English. "Exactly what does your name mean in English?" he asked again.

Both girls looked puzzled a moment, then Hong sighed.

"We no speak English too good," she said softly. "We only here six months." Her pronunciation was horrible. Even Danny, who was very used to his parents' and grandmother's thick accents, had a hard time understanding her.

"Her name mean rose," a voice said from behind them. Danny turned and saw Sang Le leaning on the swinging door. "Perfect name. She beautiful like rose." His eyes, made even more bright by the beer he had consumed, glowed as he looked at the taller girl. She blushed again.

"Her name—" he glanced at Cuc, "—mean

that yellow flower," he pointed to a bouquet of yellow and white flowers on the family altar. "How you say in English?"

"Chrysanthemum," Danny said as he twisted around and glanced at the flowers.

Cuc frowned, looped her arm through her sister's, and pulled her away from Sang Le into the living room. They sat down beside some young children playing a card game.

"That girl is so beautiful," Sang Le said, reverting back to his native language. "I'm in love with her, cousin. How graceful and shy, like a rose bending in the wind." He sighed. "Do you know her well?"

"No, I've only spoken to her once, at the market. She lives with her uncle, who works with my father. So you like her, huh?" Danny jabbed an elbow into his cousin's side and felt the ribs protruding. Sang Le shrugged and nodded, then grinned.

"Maybe you can find out something about her for me, please. A girl that beautiful has probably already had her marriage arranged to a wealthy man."

Danny laughed. "Sang Le, they don't have arranged marriages in America. People marry who they want to. They marry who they fall in love with. And most girls don't get married while they're still in high school. She's only about sixteen."

"Please, Duong, find out something about her for me."

Danny was tired and uncomfortably full from sampling all the foods. He wanted to slip into his room and lie down and look at Tiffany Marie's photograph, to get away from all the noise and people. But he thought about all the hardships his cousin had been through. What were a few minutes of his time compared to a lifetime in re-education camp? Danny shrugged.

"Sure. Come with me."

"No, no. It is better that someone else ask her. It would be rude for me to speak to her of my feelings. Find out if she is already promised to another man."

Danny started to open his mouth. Sang Le hadn't listened to a thing he had said.

Danny worked his way through the group of kids while Sang Le returned to the circle of men, where he was expected to sit as the guest of honor. It didn't seem to matter that he was not yet eighteen, that in America he wasn't old enough to vote or drink or drive a car in some states. Here he was a man. A man who had suffered through the worst of times like others there at the circle. They had not invited Danny to sit with them, nor the other teenage boy who was at the party.

In a way Danny felt insulted that he was not a part of the men's world, yet in a way he was relieved. Now, as it often did, the conversation turned to Vietnam, to the war, to the communists. He never knew from one minute to the next if one of the men might break into a patriotic song or recite lines from the national epic poem of Vietnam, or weep, or grow violent and start a fight.

Danny remembered very little about Vietnam. He had been born after the war and left when he was six. His worst memory only haunted him once in a while, like the time his American sponsor, Mr. MacIntyre, took him to Galveston and they boarded a fishing boat at night. The rocking boat, the dark waves, had suddenly filled his heart with blind terror and flashes of memory—his mother's arms squeezing him and baby Kim against her trembling body as a large boat sliced through the dark water, closer and closer until he could smell the diesel fuel and hear the sailors talking. Only much later, when he was ten, did he learn that they had fled Vietnam at night on a small fishing boat. They could not use any light, not even a cigarette lighter, for fear of being spotted, and a communist naval vessel had almost cut them in two.

Danny pushed the memory back. He didn't want to remember anything about Vietnam—that was gone, no longer part of his life. He wanted to be an American now, yet he didn't feel part of the world of the children, either. They spoke perfect English with no accents and played popular music and American games like Monopoly and Uno. They worried about clothes and friends and school lessons. The war in Vietnam was not even a pale memory, but a history lesson to be studied in school alongside their American friends.

Danny stepped over a toddler sleeping on a quilt pallet and eased into an open spot between the two sisters. He felt the hot glare of Cuc's black eyes boring into him as he settled down between them.

"Hi, I'm Danny Vo. Haven't I seen you at school?" he asked in Vietnamese, hoping to break the ice.

"Of course," Cuc snapped. "We play on the tennis court the same time as you in P.E. class sometimes. You chased our tennis ball once. Didn't you see us?" Her Vietnamese came in bursts of rising and falling monosyllables that exploded from her small lips. Danny was hardly able to follow her words, but her lowered dark eyebrows and firm chin spoke a language of their own.

Danny felt the heat creeping up his neck. He wanted to jump up and say forget you, but from the corner of his eye he saw Sang Le watching him, so he shrugged and forced a smile.

"Well, I thought I recognized you when I saw you at Di-Ho Market this morning. I'm a sophomore. How about you, Hong?"

Avoiding eye contact, the girl glanced down at her hands resting in her lap. They were small, delicately tapered, and tipped with sensible nails, just long enough to be graceful, but short enough to be practical.

"We are both in ESL class," Hong replied in a soft voice. Unlike her sister's, Hong's Vietnamese was smooth and melodic, almost like poetry. "We both study freshman classes even though Cuc is seventeen and I am sixteen. After we learn English better, maybe we will be promoted to another grade." Her large eyes lifted for a second and looked into Danny's face, then quickly glanced away.

"Okay, then let's speak English, so you can get some practice."

"Good," Cuc said in English. "Hong need more than my."

Danny held in the urge to laugh at the short

girl's awful pronunciation. But maybe his own parents had sounded just as terrible when they first came to America, so he nodded and gave her a wink.

"Good. Hong, maybe sometime you and my cousin Sang Le can go to the movies or to the mall."

"No, no, no!" Cuc shook her head. "Never she go out with boy alone. My uncle very strict. No boys. No American dancing. No bad movies." She wagged her finger savagely in his face.

Danny saw the corner of Hong's lips droop. He wished Cuc would let her sister speak for herself. But Hong was obviously intolerably shy, and she made him feel uncomfortable. He smiled and shrugged.

"Okay, I tried," he muttered. With a grunt, he struggled to his feet. "Say, Hong, you aren't engaged to be married, are you?"

She didn't understand and Cuc, who had a slightly better command of English, quickly translated. Hong broke into giggles, covered her mouth with a delicate hand, and shook her head.

Cuc squinted as she glared into Danny's face, a sure sign of rudeness. "Why you ask so many questions? Are you working for CIA?"

Danny didn't reply but shook his head and walked back to the living room. Sang Le followed him with his eyes, but didn't get up. Danny worked his way to the hallway. He was dead tired and couldn't wait to lie down. Just as he had thought, his own bed had two sleeping babies on it and his parents' bed held a sleeping man who'd had too much to drink. He rapped softly on Kim's door. Her radio was still playing, but not as loudly as before.

"Kimmy? Is anybody in there? I need a place to crash for a little while."

"Kim doesn't answer," a small girl's voice said. Danny looked down into the disgruntled face of his youngest sister. "I want to change clothes. See, I spilled orange juice all over my blouse. But Kim won't answer the door."

"Has she been locked in here ever since the fight with Bà?"

"No, I saw her go in the bathroom a couple of hours ago. Then she went back into the room and locked the door. She makes me so mad. She doesn't have the right to lock me out. My stuff is in there, too." Lan banged the door with her small fist.

"She probably cried herself to sleep. You know how hard it is to wake her up. I'll go around to the window and climb in. You wait here at the door."

Danny was glad to get out of the stuffy, hot

apartment. Outside, the misty night air felt refreshing on his face. The rain had stopped and the air was cool and clean. For a few seconds he stood still, breathing in the aroma of grilled pork and tangy lemon grass and dying charcoal from the smoldering hibachi. He carefully climbed up a bare-limbed oak tree until he was even with Kim's window. It wasn't the first time she had locked herself in the room, so he knew exactly which window to tap on. Kim did not respond.

With a grunt, he leaned over and tugged at the window. It was unlatched and moved in his hands easily. A funny feeling swept over him.

"Oh, no, Kim, don't tell me," he muttered under his breath as his hands pushed the window up the rest of the way. He lowered his body into the room and flipped on the light. The bed was empty.

"Oh, brother." Danny groaned. He tiptoed to the door and opened it just a crack.

"Kim's asleep," he lied to Lan. "What blouse do you want? I'll get it for you."

"The yellow one with the blue flowers."

"Okay . . . wait here." He opened the closet, rummaged for the blouse, then handed it through the door to his little sister.

"Don't bother Kim. She'll come out later," he said as he stepped into the hall and closed the door behind him. The door locked shut again.

Danny stood for a moment, gathering in the scene around him. He couldn't go far without a car, and his mother's car was in the shop. Only his father could give him permission to drive, but his father would want to know why and where he was going.

He walked to the kitchen. "Má, I need some fresh air. Don't you need something from the grocery store? More shrimp? More limes or bean sprouts?"

His grandmother eyed him with suspicion, but his mother made a quick survey of the table and the living room. "Sure," she replied. "We need more Cokes and some more French bread." She rummaged through her purse and took out several bills.

Danny leaned over his father's shoulder and asked for the car keys, explaining about the groceries. His father's eyes were already glazed over, and he slapped Danny on the knee proudly as he explained to the others that Danny had graduated at the top of the driver's ed. class and was a good driver already. Never mind that he didn't have his full license yet. The other men nodded their approval and drank a toast to Danny's skill.

Danny started to turn but caught the look in Sang Le's eyes.

"Maybe Sang Le would like to come with me and see an American supermarket?"

"No, no, no. He must stay here with the men," Danny's father said, placing a hand on Sang Le's knee. "He has many stories to tell us about those bastard communists who have ruined our country."

"Please, excuse me," Sang Le said as he stood. "I very much like to see American market." He bowed to each man at the table, his hands pressed to his forehead in the traditional greeting.

"He'll be back soon," Danny said as he took his cousin's arm and guided him through the door and down the stairs. He prayed the fresh, cool air would help clear his cousin's head. Danny imagined Sang Le hadn't drank so much beer in a long time.

"What did the beautiful rose say?" Sang Le asked as soon as they settled into the car.

"The beautiful what?"

"Hong. The lovely girl in your living room. Is she engaged?"

"No. And believe me, with her sister standing guard over her like a bulldog, I doubt she ever will have a boyfriend. She's not even allowed to date."

Sang Le grinned. "Good. She very good girl. Perfect for me, cousin. Perfect."

Danny turned on the cassette player. The soft notes of a Vietnamese man singing a sad love song filled the car. Danny started to turn it off and play some rock music, but Sang Le touched his hand.

"Please, let's listen to this beautiful music. Do you understand the words?"

Danny shrugged. "Sort of. It's kind of corny, I think."

"No, no, it is a beautiful love song. It is the most famous song in our country, little cousin. How a young man loved a beautiful girl, but their love could never be because she was a mandarin's daughter and he was of lowly birth. He sacrificed his life for her, and only in his death did she realize she loved him truly."

"Yeah, I can see how that would be on the top forty in Vietnam," Danny said. He hated the old-fashioned music that his father and mother listened to. Ever since someone at school had called it "ching-chang" music, Danny refused to play it and avoided it whenever possible. But Sang Le closed his eyes and leaned back into the seat. Soon he was breathing the deep, even breath of sleep. But it was not a peaceful sleep. He mumbled and his legs jerked. Once he cried out so loudly, Danny jumped and accidentally swerved the car.

"Jeez, I hope this isn't the way you always sleep, cousin," he muttered under his breath as he steered the car toward the center of the downtown Vietnamese community. Some Americans called it Little Saigon, others called the whole area Chinatown, although the Chinese were not the only Asian merchants in the area.

Danny knew exactly where to go to find Kim. She had screamed and begged enough that morning about going downtown to the Chinese movies with her friends. It was a thirty-minute drive from the apartment, but this late at night the traffic would be light. With the party in full swing, his parents might not even miss them for over an hour.

Danny steered the car carefully, keeping a wary eye out for the blue-and-white police cars. He knew it wasn't very wise to be anyplace near Chinatown at night, but all the more reason to get his sister back home. There were restaurants and respectable shops and markets, but all those places took on a sinister look after dark. A brisk wind gusted between the buildings, scattering pieces of paper down the sidewalks, lodging them against cyclone fences around parking lots. Black wrought-iron burglar bars covered the windows of every single shop.

Danny scanned the sidewalks around the

Vietnamese shops and restaurants. If the movie was over, Kim might be walking down the street with her friends. More than likely she had slipped over to Queen Bee, the main Vietnamese night spot on weekends.

Already the club's parking lot was jammed full of cars, and couples dressed in expensive dresses and suits with red or white boutonnieres stood in line for the dance club. Danny drove over to the movie theater first. Just as he had thought, the last movie had already let out and the doors were locked.

"Where are you, Kimmy?" he said aloud as he turned the steering wheel again, shifted gears, and started back down the street he had just cruised. At the sound of grinding gears, Sang Le awoke and blinked, then rubbed his eyes.

"Where are we, cousin?" he asked. "This looks like Saigon."

"We're downtown now."

Sang Le read off the names of stores and advertisements written in Vietnamese on placards and on the windows. "You come all this way to buy food from the market?"

"No. We shop over by the apartment. I'm looking for my sister, Kim." Danny quickly explained that Kim had gone to the movies with her friends, but he couldn't bring himself to tell

Sang Le that she had snuck out the window without permission.

"Please let me get out and walk for a while," Sang Le requested after a minute. "This reminds me of Vietnam."

"Okay, you look for her down that street toward the club. I'll circle around one more time. Kim is wearing a purple jacket and has an orange streak in her hair. You can't miss her."

Danny drove up and down the streets, going all the way to the oldest part of Chinatown, even though he didn't think she would go that far. When he returned to the area where he had dropped off his cousin, Danny recognized one of his neighbors leaning against a street lamp, smoking a cigarette. Danny rolled down the window.

"Have you seen my sister Kim?" he called out. The boy nodded and pointed toward a dark spot between buildings. Danny felt his heart leap into his throat when he saw four familiar teen-agers walking down the sidewalk. They wore black jackets with a yellow cobra on the back of each one. Sang Le was not more than ten feet behind them.

"Oh, no, not again," Danny said between gritted teeth. Then he saw a cluster of younger girls near the alley.

"Kim!" he shouted out of the window. "Get over here!" He didn't even try to disguise the anger in his voice. As Kim turned, a look of terror flashed across her face. She started to dart into the alley, but one of her friends must have advised her against it because Kim stopped. She hung her head, then turned to face her brother.

Danny didn't try to find a parking spot. He drove the old Toyota up onto the sidewalk, blocking Kim's escape in that direction. He leaped from the car, not bothering to shut off the motor or close the door.

"Little girl, you are in more trouble than you can begin to imagine," he said as he grabbed her arm. "What are you doing here? Are you that stupid? What do you think Cha will say when he finds out? I know he lets you get away with almost anything, but you've gone too far this time. He'll ground you for a month. And Bà— heaven help you when she finds out. She'll make you kneel in front of the altar until your knees rot off."

Kim's girlfriends snickered. Danny threw them an angry scowl and they got quiet.

"We're just having some harmless fun," Kim said. "I went to one little movie, Danny. It was one of those silly kung fu movies, nothing sexy. Jennifer and Brittany had never seen a Chinese movie before. Their brother drove us here. He'll pick us back up in a few minutes. We're just standing around talking. I didn't do anything wrong."

"Oh, yes you did. You disobeyed your parents. You dishonored me. I don't care if you went to a Sunday school picnic. You didn't get my permission."

"You're not my master," Kim spat out. She wiggled from his grasp by jerking her arms free from her purple jacket. When Danny saw her sheer black blouse, he quickly made her put the jacket back on.

They were at each other's throats when a soft voice interrupted.

"Is this my cousin Kim?" Sang Le asked in Vietnamese. Kim stopped and looked up.

"Yes, I'm Kim. Who are you?"

"I am your cousin Sang Le," he said. He spoke Vietnamese very slowly and deliberately, trying very hard to make Kim understand his words. "I haven't seen you since you were a tiny little girl. Do you know you were the most beautiful baby I ever saw in my life? Everyone said you were. All the while I was in re-education camp, and later when I was in refugee camp in Hong Kong, I thought about you. I would close my eyes and see your fat little cheeks and pretty dimples and try to imagine what you look like now."

Kim's hard face slowly began to soften and a little smile played at the corner of her lips. "That was nice of you, cousin Sang Le."

"All the time I was a prisoner, I thought about you and Duong and Bà and your parents, and Lan and Thuy. The thought of coming to America someday and seeing all of you was what kept me alive. I could have given up, like hundreds of others did, and lain down and died. We had little food and water, and the diseases knocked us off like flies. Others wept at night because they had no future. But not me. I talked all night long about handsome little Duong and beautiful little chubby-cheeked Kim. I pretended what I would do when I saw you again. Even after my best friend died, I had you and Duong and all your family to think about to keep my courage. Please, Kim . . . come to my welcoming party. Show me that you are as beautiful inside as you are outside."

He held his arms open and Kim melted into them. Tears slid down his face as his arms closed around her and pulled her near. He kissed the top of her orange-streaked hair.

"Thank you, little cousin," he said softly.

Kim glanced at Danny, then quickly wiped

her nose on her jacket sleeve and told her friends she had to leave.

While Kim and Sang Le crawled into the car, Danny saw the four Cobra gang members loitering at the entrance to the dance club, watching the scene. The chubby one with the flattop shouted to Danny.

"You sure got a lot of sisters, man. At least this one looks number one okay." He formed two of his fingers into an obscene gesture common among Vietnamese men.

Danny glared at them as long as he dared, then slid into the driver's seat. He didn't want to start anything with Cobra's friend, but he couldn't force himself to pretend he wasn't mad at the remark and the gesture. Just looking at Cobra made Danny's heart pump faster and the hairs on the back of his neck stand up.

"You don't know that creep Cobra, do you, Kim?" Danny asked.

"No . . . not exactly. I know Quan. His older brother is a Cobra, but he's not. He hates gangs." Her eyes focused on a handsome, muscular boy who stood slightly apart from the others—the only one who wasn't wearing a black jacket.

"Well, keep away from all those guys. They're nothing but trouble."

Kim shrugged. "Whatever," she mumbled.

Danny knew his words had fallen on deaf ears. She would never listen to him. It was Sang Le who had charmed her tonight just as he had charmed Bà earlier. Whether or not his power to persuade would last, Danny didn't know. Maybe Sang Le was just intuitive when it came to young girls and old women. Maybe he just understood people better than Danny. Or maybe he really was under the lucky shadow of a dragon.

When they got home, Danny tried to help Kim sneak in but Bà caught them. The house was in an uproar, and as predicted, Danny's father grounded Kim for a month.

"You are so much like my sister, Nga," he wailed through tears, "so full of spirit and fire. But you must use your energy for good things. Why do you break our hearts like this?"

Danny hated seeing his father cry and knew that Kim was feeling bad, too. But she remained silent and her eyes remained dry as she knelt by the altar in front of all the guests while he lectured her. She was still on her knees, her head hung, thirty minutes later when Danny got ready for bed.

He was in a deep sleep when his cousin staggered into the bedroom and woke him up. Danny wasn't sure if Sang Le was exhausted or drunk, but he gave his cousin a pair of new pajamas and showed him to the lower bunk under Thuy, who had long ago fallen into the deep sleep of little boys.

Off and on during the early morning hours, Danny heard the cries of his cousin—the whimpering, the shouts, the kicking legs and flaying arms.

"Are you all right?" Danny whispered. "Are you having bad dreams?"

Sang Le rolled over. "They are not dreams, little cousin, they are memories."

When he awoke, Danny found Sang Le on the floor without covers and his new bunk bed hardly slept in. Though it was time to get up, Danny felt exhausted and could barely force his body to move.

As Danny splashed cool water on his face, the thought occurred to him that Bà would be happy to see him in this condition. He was sleepy, he was tired, he was miserable. At last he was sacrificing for the good of the family; at last he was behaving like a true dragon-child.

Chapter Five

Waiting for the school bus on the following Monday morning, Danny's cousin acted as nervous and excited as a six year old on the first day of school. Shopping at the mall the day before, he had been the same way. Danny couldn't tell Sang Le to his face, but everything he tried on clung to his bony frame and looked like sheets hung out over a bare-limbed tree in the winter.

Shopping had taken most of the day. Sang Le was picky, but not for the reasons some people might expect. He argued with every penny spent, not wanting to take the clothes his aunt bought for him. He said he would manage with only one pair of pants and a shirt. And he truly meant what he said. Only after he had looked inside the closet Danny shared with his little brother, did Sang Le begin to realize that one set of clothes would not do in America.

So when Danny and his cousin climbed on the bus that morning, Sang Le blended into the crowd very well.

Calvin Pickney was already in his favorite seat toward the middle of the bus. Only the bravest souls dared to sit in the far back where the pot heads and boozers snored off their week-end hangovers or slipped their hands all over the willing, easy girls.

Calvin gave that disgusted look that Danny knew so well, with his full lips forming a down-ward frown. Danny had avoided talking to him all weekend. The burden of buying the solar pack for their science project had fallen into Dan-ny's hands and he had failed miserably. The coming-home party, going to the market, to the airport, to the mall, all those things were mere excuses. Danny had known about all that when he agreed to buy the solar battery.

"Where's the solar pack?" Calvin asked as Danny slid in beside him.

"Cal, this is my cousin Sang Le from Viet-nam."

"Hi, Shane Lee," Calvin said, then turned back to Danny. "Well?"

"We had Sang Le's homecoming party this weekend."

"You didn't get it, did ya?"

"You know how parties are, Cal, you can't get anything done."

"Hmph!" Calvin had a way with words, no doubt about it. "My sister Lashandra had her birthday party this weekend, too."

"Yeah? How old is your charming sister?" The image of Calvin's bossy and not exactly petite sister flashed across Danny's mind.

"Eighteen. Her party didn't stop me from doing my part of the project. Without that battery, how are we going to finish up in time? You let me down, man." Calvin slumped back into the seat and hissed air between his teeth.

"I'm sorry, Cal . . . something else happened, too. Kim . . ." Danny wanted to tell him about Kim taking off but figured it would be better to keep that part of the weekend secret. Even though Calvin was his best friend, Danny was embarrassed to have him know that Kim was out of control.

"You could have at least answered my phone call," Calvin blurted out. "You didn't have to tell your sister to lie about you not being there when you really were."

"I wasn't lying. When did you call?"

" 'Bout seven o'clock Saturday night."

"I *was* there at seven o'clock. Wait a minute, which sister?"

"Which sister you got that's always on the telephone every time I call?"

"Kim?"

"Uh-huh," Calvin nodded. He flashed a grin and held up his index finger. "That's the one."

"Well, she lied, Cal. I swear, she lied. I was home then. She just didn't want to give up the telephone, and I know why. She must have been making plans with her skinny-butt friends. She snuck out with them and went downtown."

"That Kim is about the sneakiest girl I've ever met. Guess you did have your hands full."

Danny glanced at the street corner where the junior high kids were gathered for their bus. Kim's skinny legs stuck out of her oversized coat like toothpicks. The weatherman's prediction had finally come true and a cold front had moved through during the night, leaving it frigid. Frost billowed from Kim's mouth as she laughed and danced a jig to keep warm.

Sang Le had to sit directly behind Danny and Cal. The bus was jam-packed because of the cold weather. On nice days some of the guys skipped school and hung around or went to Galveston. Winters never were much in Houston, mostly no more than a couple of days below freezing. The cold days would be gone by the middle of March and then the hot, humid days of summer would slip in almost overnight, with no spring to speak of.

Danny introduced his cousin to a couple of his neighbors. Cal didn't understand a word Sang Le said. Neither did most of the Americans on the bus. Only the other Vietnamese and one Cambodian who had lived in Vietnam could grasp his accent. Danny heard a few snickers from a seat of girls behind him. They were probably laughing at Sang Le, but Danny chose to ignore them. And poor Sang Le was too frustrated to notice he was being laughed at.

"Why nobody understand my?" he asked as they stepped off the bus. "I practice English six months in refugee camp. All day. My teacher very, very good. She work for American Army five year." He held up five fingers.

Danny shrugged. "You just need more practice. Don't worry about it. You'll be speaking perfect English just like that." Danny snapped his fingers. Sang Le burst into a smile and nodded.

"Okay, cousin."

As usual, as soon as Danny stepped off the bus, his eyes made a beeline for bus number 133. That was Tiffany Marie's bus. All the while Sang Le talked to him, spilling his soul about studying English in the refugee camp, Danny was searching for the blond hair, blue eyes, and neat clothes that would mark her appearance. Tiffany didn't just step off the bus, she bounced like a frisky kitten. Danny's heart almost stopped when he finally saw her, smiling and laughing as always with some girlfriend.

It had been one of God's greatest gifts that Tiffany and Danny had shared at least one class together since eighth grade. This year it was the first class of the day, American history. It had taken Danny all of those three years to get to the point where they spoke at their lockers and in class occasionally. She sat near the front and Danny sat near the back. This was a great arrangement. Danny could see her every move and she couldn't see him at all. His days didn't seem to start until he had seen her smile and the flip of her hair and the way her leg rocked back and forth when the teacher was going into some long, boring speech.

But today Danny had to miss all that. He told the history teacher, Mr. Carnes, about his cousin and was excused to help Sang Le register and get settled into ESL—English as a Second Language. Danny took his cousin first to the main office. The initial paperwork seemed to take forever, then they walked to the ESL classroom, located at the far end of the school in some temporary buildings up on concrete cinder blocks. Danny didn't mind missing history class—Mr. Carnes was his least favorite teacher—but he hated missing Tiffany Marie.

As they walked down the halls, Sang Le lingered at every open door, glancing in and asking what kind of class it was. The more weird the things he saw, the more questions he asked. Maps, globes, the chemistry lab, the biology class with a skeleton dangling near the door, the computer class, and the home economics class with its stifling burnt-toast smell. Nothing missed Sang Le's sharp eyes.

The minute they stepped into the ESL room, thirty-five pairs of brown eyes turned toward them. Danny recognized some students from P.E. class—Nicaraguans and El Salvadorans and Colombians. But by far the greatest majority came from Mexico. Ms. Rodriguez smiled a big smile, emphasized by bright red lipstick. She thanked Danny, read over the papers he had handed her, and pulled Sang Le to the front of the class.

"Students, this is Ly Le Sang. He's just come

to the United States from Vietnam. Please say, Hello, Ly."

"Hello, Ly," the class repeated in unison as if they were reciting multiplication tables.

Danny cleared his throat. "Uh, Ms. Rodriguez, Ly is his last name. His first name is Sang; his middle name is Le. In Vietnam, they put the last name first."

"Oh, of course. How silly of me to forget."

"And it's pronounced 'shang.'"

Danny squeezed his cousin's arm and whispered in Vietnamese, "Good luck, cousin. I'll see you at lunchtime. We have the same break. Don't forget, our bus is number 21."

Danny felt his cousin's body stiffen as he started to walk away. Sang Le's Adam's apple bobbed as he swallowed hard.

"Just relax, don't be nervous." Danny placed a hand on Sang Le's shoulder. "Look, I see somebody you know in the back row."

Sang Le's eyes searched the rows of faces, then suddenly a smile burst across his face.

"It is beautiful rose and her sister," Sang Le whispered back, his eyes shining. "I have good luck already today."

Danny winked at his cousin. "You won't have any problems. They'll show you everything." Danny waved good-bye and started back down the hall, going as fast as he could without breaking into an actual trot. His sneakers tapped and squeaked on the shiny waxed floors. From every open door, sleepy, glazed-over eyes turned as Danny hurried by.

Just as Danny rounded the corner near his history classroom, the bell sounded and a wave of students flowed from the rooms to the lockers, blocking his view of the door.

"Shoot!" Danny muttered as he pushed his way toward his locker. He grabbed the books for his morning classes and scoured the hall for Tiffany. He saw her blond hair and pale pink jumpsuit vanishing around the corner. With a curse, he slammed his fist into the locker.

That was the way it went all day. If Danny was coming out of a room, Tiffany was going in. If she was going up the stairs, Danny was going down the stairs. Lunch period became his sole reason for existing. Danny knew that he would be able at least to admire her from a distance then.

When she walked through the cafeteria doors, his heart did somersaults and the blood rushed to his face. Danny watched her get a tray and move down the line, looking delicate and fragile between Billy Bracken, star fullback, and Luther Jones, a six-foot center for the basketball team. She got a salad and dessert then found a table in the far corner. She opened up a paperback book and began reading. Nobody was sitting next to her. It would have been the perfect opportunity for Danny to talk to her.

"Uh-oh, look who's coming through the door," Calvin said with a wink. Danny tore his eyes from Tiffany and looked up.

Sang Le was creeping through the double doors, looking like a puppy lost in a rainstorm.

"Yo, coz, over here," Calvin stood up and shouted at the top of his lungs. Everyone, including Tiffany Marie, turned.

Sang Le's face lit up and Danny could hear his sigh of relief from across the room as the slender boy hurried to join them. All his childlike enthusiasm of the morning had vanished. Welcome to the real world, Danny wanted to say.

The cafeteria had hamburgers that day. Well, Danny guessed it was supposed to be Salisbury steaks, but it was really hamburger patties buried under a layer of gooey brown stuff. If it hadn't been for the fruit section of the line, Danny didn't think Sang Le would have eaten anything at all. He looked like it was an effort to keep from throwing up on the spot. He didn't want any dessert, either. Like Bà and Danny's parents, Sang Le had little taste for sweets other than fruits.

"So, how was your first day of American school?" Danny asked him.

Sang Le released a ragged sigh, then took a deep drink of orange juice.

"That bad, huh?" Calvin said.

Sang Le quickly forced a smile. "No, no, American school number one." He held up an index finger. "Very good teacher. I learn fast. All teacher very good." He bobbed his head up and down as if to emphasize each sentence.

"Great. I'm glad somebody in the family is having a good day." As Danny spoke he watched Tiffany across the room. She continued to sit alone, her head buried in the paperback. She wasn't being unfriendly, Danny knew that. She was probably reading an English literature assignment. The only person she spoke to was a sloppy-looking, big-boned guy with hair shaved close around the edges, leaving a tiny strip of curly blond hair on top. The hairstyle made his head seem too small for his broad shoulders and pudgy stomach.

"Who's that creep talking to your dream girl?" Calvin whispered.

Danny shrugged. "I've seen him talking to her before. Believe it or not, I think that's her brother. Otherwise, I can't imagine why she would be anywhere near him." Tiffany wasn't smiling or laughing. She kept a quiet, drawn expression on her face and nodded as the boy spoke. As soon as he walked away, she buried her nose in her book again.

"Wait a minute, I remember that guy." Calvin snapped his fingers. "He entered the science fair two years ago. Man, he really got mad when he came in third place. That was the year Trung Tran won, and that big bag of blubber almost jumped down Trung's throat."

"That's right, I remember now. Well, Trung is a genius anyway. Nobody can ever beat his projects."

"I'll find out if he's Tiffany's brother," Calvin volunteered and leaped up from the table, scraping his metal chair across the floor as he rose.

"Cal!" Danny cringed as his friend swaggered toward the lunch line where the big teenager was talking to two other boys who looked even worse than he did. At least he had a fringe on top of his head; theirs were completely shaven. And their clothes looked like something you might have dug out of the reject pile behind the Goodwill Store. Danny didn't hear what the boys said to Calvin, but whatever it was sent him scurrying back, his head low and his mouth turned down again.

"Well?" Danny asked.

"Forget that creep."

"But who is he?"

"I didn't get his name and don't care. He's a skinhead, man. So prejudiced he can't see any color but his own. You'd better stay away from him if you're smart. He's got the meanest little weasely eyes I've ever seen." Calvin slurped his soda straw *ad nauseam*.

Sang Le quickly flipped through the pages of his tiny English-to-Vietnamese dictionary, which was concealed behind a larger book, as if he were embarrassed to be seen looking up words.

" 'Skin-head' not in dictionary," he whispered to Danny. "How you say in Vietnamese?"

Danny shrugged. "It means he has no hair on top of his head."

"And no brains on top, either," Calvin muttered as he jabbed his fork into the mashed potatoes.

"But I don't see how Tiffany Schultz could have a skinhead brother, Cal," Danny said after watching the tall boy and his friends sit at a table across the room. "You must be wrong."

"Maybe he's not her brother. Maybe he was asking her for the time. Or trying to hit on her. Anyhow, believe me, he's a genuine Nazi. Come on, let's go. This place is making me sick all of a sudden."

Danny showed Sang Le where to meet after school, then walked with Calvin to P.E. class. Danny never could get Calvin to tell exactly what the big, blond-haired boy said to him, or maybe it had been one of the other two guys. It must have been really personal, because Calvin wasn't one to keep secrets from Danny.

By last period, which was physics class, Calvin's uneasiness over whatever had been said was replaced by his uneasiness over their floundering science project. The teacher, as usual, reminded the class when it was due and how much the grade would count and how you wouldn't be able to pass physics unless you got a passing grade on the project and how the best ones would be entered in the citywide science fair.

Danny knew the teacher would like their project. It was a miniature house, built from scratch. Everything in it would be powered by energy-efficient mechanisms. The lights, which were tiny Christmas lights, would be powered by a solar cell—the one Danny had forgotten to buy. The water was heated by tiny solar panels on top of the roof, miniatures of the ones on top of Calvin's house. And the miniature ceiling fans would be powered by an outdoor wind generator, if they could ever get it to work. That had been their biggest hang-up. That and painstakingly designing all the pieces of metal and wood to build the house. Putting it together was going to be tedious, but Lashandra's old dollhouse furniture would fit inside it perfectly. Of course, *she* didn't know that yet.

Danny couldn't remember a longer day. By the time he was at his locker after the final bell sounded, cramming books in and taking out others, Danny was brain-dead. The only thing that kept his eyes open was knowing that this would be his last chance to talk to Tiffany. He saw her pink jumpsuit coming down the hall and stalled. He buried his head in his notebook, pretending to check over his assignments.

"Hi, Danny." Her voice floated over the five feet between their lockers. "I missed you in history today. Did you miss the bus or something?"

"No. I had to help my cousin get enrolled in ESL class. It took a long time."

"Oh, was he the boy sitting next to you and Calvin Pickney at lunchtime?"

Danny's face suddenly felt hot and his hands were dripping sweat. He nodded. "Yes. He's just over from Hong Kong."

"Hong Kong? Is he Chinese?"

"No, he was . . . well, in a refugee camp there for a while."

"A refugee camp. That sounds awful, Danny.

I'm so glad he's in America now. I bet he's happy to be with his family." Her blue eyes shimmered, expressing more than just concern for a foreigner she'd never met. Something else was there; Danny knew he wasn't imagining things. She always waved at him on the tennis courts, or if she saw him at the mall or driving down her street.

Danny swallowed hard and tried to think of something really cool to say. Now was the perfect time to set up a date for next weekend. She looked so pretty and so genuinely glad to see him that a wave of courage washed over him.

"Uh, Tiffany . . ." Danny cleared his throat and started to speak, but before the rest of the sentence came out, Tiffany suddenly looked at someone behind him. Danny felt a skinny hand rest on his shoulder.

"*Chao anh,* cousin," Sang Le said. "Bus number 21. I remember." He glanced at Tiffany and bowed, his dark eyes full of wonder and approval. "Is this your girlfriend?" he quickly asked in Vietnamese.

"No," Danny said in English. "Tiffany, this is my cousin, Sang Le. The one I told you about. Sang Le, this is Tiffany Marie Schultz."

"It is a pleasure to make your acquaintance, beautiful lady," Sang Le said in his best English and grabbed her hand. He shook it up and down hard in exaggerated motions and grinned. Tiffany had a blank expression on her face. Her eyebrows twisted as she concentrated on the garbled words tumbling from the boy's lips. Even Danny didn't catch all of what his cousin said.

"Welcome to America, Sang Le," she finally said, a big smile on her face.

"You number one chick," Sang Le said loudly.

As Tiffany broke into laughter, Danny felt the heat oozing up his neck to his ears. Why had Sang Le chosen this particular moment to try out everything he had learned in ESL class that day? Danny looped an arm through his cousin's and gently tugged him away. "Uh, he still needs a lot of practice."

"No, no, he's doing great," she said. "My grandparents emigrated from Germany. I know English is a hard language to learn. Right, Sang Le?"

He nodded, though Danny doubted he understood her, either. A long painful silence followed. Tiffany's face suddenly clouded over and her eyes opened wide.

"Oh, I've gotta go now. There's my brother Frank. He promised me a ride home today. We've got to run some errands for Mom. See you later, Danny. Good luck, Sang Le." She touched Danny's arm lightly. She had done that to him once before. It felt like a butterfly landing on his arm, so delicate and light. Her nails, though chewed to the quick, were painted pale pink to match her jumpsuit. Danny's eyes followed her down the hall and watched her meet the same big-boned, blond-haired guy he had seen in the lunchroom.

Even though his suspicions had been confirmed that he was her brother, Danny still found it hard to believe that the guy was really a skinhead. Surely a family that had produced such a terrific girl had produced a nice son, too, in spite of his shaved head and weird clothes and the crowd he hung out with. Sometimes things like that happened. Like the difference between Danny and Kim. Besides, even if Frank *was* a skinhead, his sister obviously wasn't prejudiced.

As he watched Tiffany vanish around the corner, a wave of self-disgust swept over him. "I almost did it," Danny said aloud. "I came that close to asking her out." He slammed the locker door, then slapped it with his open palm. He let out a scream of frustration.

Sang Le stood by, his head hung. If he had been wearing a hat, he would have been holding it in his hand, twisting the rim. "Sorry, cousin. I do something wrong?" he asked softly.

Danny took a deep breath and counted to eight, his lucky number. "Of course not. We'd better hurry or we'll miss the bus."

A few minutes later they settled down next to Calvin. This time there was plenty of room because some of the kids had left school early for jobs or their parents had picked them up or they had gotten rides with friends.

"Hey, I found out who that big, dumb blond guy hanging around Tiffany Schultz is," Danny said as he plopped down and jammed his feet on the seat in front of him. "He definitely is her brother."

"Ah, too bad, Dan-O," Calvin chirped. "Like father, like son; like brother, like sister."

"No way. She's nothing like him. She's perfect, man. Perfect."

Sang Le may not have understood every word Cal and Danny were saying, but he must have gotten the gist of it, because suddenly he leaned over and said, in fairly clear English, "Tiffany very pretty girl, cousin. But better you marry Vietnamese girl. American girl trouble."

Danny nearly choked he laughed so hard. "Sang Le, you sound just like Bà. I've heard those very words from her lips."

"Our grandmother very wise. She very old. She learn many things from life."

Danny nearly spat out his chewing gum

when he heard that line. Even Calvin started giggling. He'd had a few brushes with Bà, too. Mostly she glared at him and made remarks about his black skin and wondered why he didn't just wash the color off. She considered him almost as unlucky a sign as the neighbor's cat.

"So, Sang Le," Danny said after catching his breath. "How were your afternoon classes? What do you think of America now?"

Sang Le's face remained still for a long time, then he drew in his breath and forced a smile.

"I must be patient. Nothing of value comes easy. Nothing." He turned his head and pressed his nose against the windowpane.

As the bus bumped over a deep pothole that jarred their teeth, Danny grew silent, also. He thought about Tiffany and how much he wanted her. Maybe his cousin's advice was meant for him, too.

Chapter Six

Tet, the Vietnamese Lunar New Year, arrived that year exactly two weeks after Sang Le's plane had landed in America. Unlike the western New Year, which always comes on January 1 no matter what, the Asian Lunar New Year fluctuates from year to year because the ancient Chinese calendar uses phases of the moon to determine the length of the year. Tet begins on the second new moon after the winter solstice, usually sometime between January 20 and February 20. Traditionally it lasts two weeks until the first full moon, but in America most Vietnamese only celebrate the first three days.

Occasionally, Tet coincides with a day important to any teenager in love—St. Valentine's Day. As luck would have it, Tet arrived that year on Friday, February 14, the same night that Danny's high school was hosting its annual Valentine's Day dance in the gymnasium.

Danny tried not to think about the dance. He wasn't the world's greatest dancer, but he had put up with Calvin's weird gyrations and learned a few slow steps from Aunt Lien, who was an expert ballroom dancer, just in case Tiffany Marie said she would go with him. Danny had bought tickets when a sudden wave of courage and faith swept over him after the announcement was made about the dance. He wanted to buy tickets before they sold out, even though he wasn't sure he'd have the nerve to ask Tiffany to go with him. And having the tickets in hand might encourage him to ask her.

Danny's household during Tet season was always hectic. His American friends never could understand why a New Year was considered so important. When Danny was younger he tried to explain to them that Tet was more than just a celebration of the coming new year. It was the biggest event of the year for Chinese and Vietnamese people. It marked the arrival of spring and the hope of a new rice crop to the farmers.

It was more like Christmas, New Year's, Thanksgiving, and your birthday all rolled up into one.

On New Year's Day, every Vietnamese man, woman, and child is considered to be one year older, no matter what month he or she was born in. Individual birthdays are only for one-year-old children. The day of your birth is far less important than the day of your death. A person's death day, *ma gio,* is celebrated by family members for many years to come.

Danny found that trying to explain this to American kids, who love grand birthday parties, was almost fruitless. Most of his Vietnamese friends saw a great opportunity to celebrate twice. They celebrated their traditional Vietnamese birthday at Tet and received gifts, but often convinced their parents to have an "American" birthday party on the day they were born, too. This wasn't much of a problem. Danny never met a Vietnamese family that didn't like to throw a party. And more than likely, there would be just as many adults at the birthday party as there were children. The occasion didn't seem to matter—birthday, homecoming, Christmas, New Year, death day, birth of a baby, whatever—eating, drinking, games, and friendship were the same.

Bà was floating on a cloud of happiness. Her tiny twig of *hoa mai* had produced three pitifully small, puny-looking buds. If they opened at all it would be a miracle. But this did not dampen Bà's high spirits or hopes. Every day it was the same routine for her. First she would check the water level, then she would move the vase to a spot with the proper light, then later in the day she would move it to a part of the apartment where it was cooler. If Danny's little brother or sister came within three feet of it while playing or studying, she broke into the same hysterical patter.

"Shh, shh, get away from *hoa mai,*" she would say. "You must be careful. If it blooms on the first day of Tet, we will have double good luck all year."

"Bà, that thing isn't going to bloom. Look at how scrawny it is," Danny said on Thursday, the thirteenth of February, while he crammed for a history exam. Danny needed the whole kitchen table to spread out his notes and books.

"Don't say that. Bad spirits will hear you and make it so," she whined in her high-pitched, singsong voice. "You must be very good and courteous so the Kitchen God, Ong Tao, will give a good report to the Jade Emperor in

Heaven. This table is too messy. He will tell the Jade Emperor that I am a bad housekeeper and punish us all year."

She started closing his books and scooting papers into neat little stacks. She replaced the offering bowl of fruits, a tiny pot of honey, and some paper clothing that she had so carefully arranged in the middle of the table as bribes for Ong Tao. Above the table hung a paper fish, a carp, for the plump and freshly gorged Kitchen God to ride back to Heaven with a good report if he liked the treats.

"Bà!" Danny said with a sigh. "You're messing up my papers. I need those books. The kitchen is spotless. I could eat off the floor, it's so clean. You and Má and Kim have been working for days to make the place look great. Ong Tao won't give you a bad report just because I'm studying on the table. He's not stupid, is he?"

"Hush, grandson. If you make fun of Ong Tao, you will have double, triple bad luck all year. Please obey your elders and show him you are a good boy. The spirits of your ancestors are watching you. They come to earth during Tet every year. We must have their tombs ready and a clean house for them. We must wear new clothes and use new chopsticks. We must pay off our debts so we will not have to borrow during the coming year. We must be good and happy, so all the year we will be good and happy."

"Bà," Lan said as she ran her finger over the rim of a china plate filled with strips of sweetened winter melon and colored coconut, "if Great-Grandma's and Great-Grandpa's spirits are coming to earth at Tet, how will they find us? Aren't their tombs in Vietnam?"

"Yes, their tombs are in our ancestral cemetery outside the beautiful city of Hue. That is where your grandfather is buried, too. I should be there beside him. I have lived too long already." She heaved a long, ragged sigh and her black eyes glistened. But she wasn't fooling Danny. Often she changed the subject whenever one of the children asked her a logical question about spirits or ghosts or one of her thousand-and-one superstitions or the strange, foul-smelling jars of herbal home remedies that she kept in the hall closet.

"Well, Bà," Danny asked, "how *do* the spirits manage to visit the ancestral tombs in Vietnam at the same time they are visiting us here in America? Split personalities, maybe?"

"Shh, don't talk bad about spirits. I saw plenty of ghosts in Vietnam. One of them jumped right on our house roof one night. He made my baby brother get sick and die."

Lan's eyes grew larger. Danny rolled his.

"If you are not good children, bad spirits will come in the night and steal your breath away," Bà continued.

"I thought only cats do that," Danny said.

"Cats are bad spirits in disguise. That cat next door is the worst bad spirit I ever saw. He made my onions get rotten roots. I saw him digging in there. Next day, my onions died." She threw her hands up and made a "poof" sound.

"Hmm, I don't suppose the ten inches of rain in three days had anything to do with the rotten roots," Danny muttered, then cracked his pencil down hard on the Formica tabletop. It was pointless to try to study in the kitchen. He had been a fool to think he could get anything done.

As Danny folded his books and scooped his papers together, his little sister leaned over and spoke into his ear. "Danny, why are you so mean to Bà? If you aren't nice, she won't give you any *li-xi*."

Danny looked down into Lan's smooth, heart-shaped face. He would have said the very same words himself a few years ago. Always that threat of not getting any *li-xi* money at Tet hung over a child's head. But even worse than that was the threat of bringing the family bad luck the coming year. If a child misbehaved during

Tet, the evil spirits would punish the family with a sickness, or a broken car radiator, or some other catastrophe. In theory, the principle worked both ways. Parents were supposed to be perfectly wonderful to their children during Tet, too. Angry words to a child could bring the bad luck just as swiftly as an unruly child could.

A feeling of affection moved over Danny as he looked into his sister's sweet, innocent face. In her blue jeans and Minnie Mouse sweater, she looked one hundred percent American. Yet her questions about spirits and ancestral tombs could have been asked by a nine year old in Saigon or Hanoi.

Danny watched Lan put her arms around Bà's frail, bony shoulders. He had not done that for a very long time, but he knew what the old woman's body felt like, as thin and light as a dried tree limb.

"Bà, who is going to be our first guest of the New Year?" he asked. "Have you decided who to ask?"

Her old eyes lit up and she dove into her reply. "Oh, I am so undecided. I had planned to ask Dr. Bui who lives three blocks away. He knew my husband in Hue. They were children together and attended the same schools. He even petted an imperial elephant once. But his father died three months ago. He is not going to visit anyone's house for fear of bringing bad luck. He is still in mourning and must not anger his father's spirit. Mr. Bui has not yet held the first *ma gio* ceremony that must be celebrated one hundred days after a loved one's death."

"Hmm, that's too bad. So, what about Mr. Duy?"

Bà's face flushed and a tiny smile crept to the corners of her thin lips.

"Ah, Mr. Duy would be perfect. He has no family in Houston. Only a sister in California. He is a true gentleman. Did you know he was a literature professor at the University of Saigon? He was quite famous for his poetry when he was younger. He looks good for a man of seventy-five, doesn't he? Still tall and straight and strong."

Danny glanced at Lan and winked. "I think Bà is in love," Danny whispered. Lan covered her mouth with her hands to hide her giggle. "And so it's Mr. Duy who has consented to be our first guest?" he asked.

"Perhaps. There is also Mr. Loc who owns the rice bag factory. He is a second cousin of my mother. He is very important and would come if we paid him a nice fee. I consulted the astrologer and he told me either man would be good for us this year. Of course, Mr. Loc is much younger than I am. He doesn't appreciate the old traditions like Mr. Duy."

"And not nearly as handsome and strong as Mr. Duy, right, Bà?" Danny leaned over and placed a soft kiss on top of her head. She grunted and brushed him away.

Danny took the books into his room. As usual, Sang Le was poring over his English lessons, struggling with the concept of personal pronouns, which were not used in the Vietnamese language. He was still just as likely to call a man "she" or a woman "he." Lan came into the room and patiently tried to explain the difference between *they* and *them,* with very little success.

Danny knew he wouldn't get any studying done here. His little brother was reciting some lines of poetry from *Kim Van Kieu,* the most popular of Vietnam's many famous epic poems, trying to memorize it before the Tet program Saturday in which he had a small part. It was important to Thuy, so Danny didn't bother him.

Danny checked to see if the girls' room was free, but Kim and Má were busy trying on their new *ao dai,* long tunics with snug-fitting bodices, which they would wear to the New Year's program at the Distinguished Vietnamese Citizens Center. Kim wasn't very excited. She was still grounded from her episode the night of Sang Le's arrival two weeks ago. At least she still respected the New Year traditions and *tried* to be on her best behavior during Tet. Maybe she was only pretending to be interested, but thank goodness for her ability to act decent for a change.

In the living room, Danny's father and uncle and a friend were arguing about something. Like many of his Asian co-workers, Cha was using part of his annual vacation time for the holiday.

"Duong," his father called. "Please come here and translate this for me." He held an official document in one hand and a Vietnamese-English dictionary in the other. Danny sighed. Sometimes translating the simplest piece of paper turned into a major issue. Even though Danny could read the English words, he couldn't always make sense of them, like the time he had had to translate the apartment lease. He was only twelve years old then, but the only family member who read English well. And when his father had to go to traffic court, it was Danny who missed school and went with him to translate what the judge said and vice versa. Once he filled out his mother's worker's compensation papers after she had an accident at the sewing factory. He was fourteen that year.

If he was lucky it would just be another

contest, one of those "You have won a million dollars" packets that Uncle Dao was always getting so excited about. Danny picked up the stapled papers. It was some legal mumbo-jumbo from his father's employer about pensions and IRA rollovers and retirement funds. After reading the first paragraph, Danny ran his fingers through his hair and groaned. This was even worse than income tax forms. He tried to explain what he was reading, but the men stared at him with blank faces.

"Cha, I don't know exactly what all this means," Danny finally said. "I'll show this to Calvin's father tomorrow. He's an accountant."

"Someday I will learn English better," Danny's father grumbled as he took the papers back. "It isn't right for a father to depend on his children for such important matters. It is I who should be guiding them. My boss said I could become a supervisor if I would learn to speak English better. I could get a raise. But when do I have time to take classes? I work all the time."

Danny left the men arguing about the meaning of "IRA rollover" and went to the only peaceful place he could find—the large outdoor concrete landing that served as a patio. Cars zoomed by on the street below, or slowed for the red light at the nearby intersection. During warmer weather, the patio was the focal point for his father, uncle, and their friends every evening after work. They would eat and drink and talk and watch the world below. Although there must have been close to a hundred thousand Vietnamese in the city, Danny swore his father and uncle knew every single Vietnamese who drove by.

Danny scooted a plastic chair up to the guardrail and propped his feet on it, then flipped open his history book. His class was studying the Vietnam War. He knew a few of the things, like the names of towns, but if he relied on his parents' and Bà's version of the war, Danny knew he would flunk the test for sure. After half an hour of reading—he was on the paragraph about the Tet Offensive of 1968, the battle that destroyed Bà's home in Hue and forced her to move to Da Nang—Danny fell into a deep sleep.

The next day, Danny crawled onto the bus, half awake. After his long nap outside, he had studied until three in the morning. Sang Le was tired, too, having studied personal pronouns until two A.M. Only Calvin's constant chatter about how far behind they were in the science project kept Danny awake. It was due Monday. Today was Friday. They had worked the kinks out of the windmill and tested the solar cell, but they would have to hit it hard and fast to put the little experimental house together. They also had to turn in a typed report of how they had proceeded with the project, step by step, with dates, failures, successes, and so forth. Danny had kept meticulous notes, but neither he nor Calvin knew how to type. They would have to bribe Lashandra to do it for them, and she drove a very hard bargain. On top of all that, Danny had a string of New Year's functions to attend and knew in his heart that he would probably get nothing done until Sunday. And that was cutting it too close for Calvin.

"Why all she wear red dress?" Sang Le asked as they walked down a hallway bustling with activity. Girls were wearing pretty pink or red dresses, stockings, and dress shoes. Some wore flower corsages, too.

After hearing an explanation of Valentine's Day, Sang Le hurried away and Calvin drilled Danny about going to the dance that night. Danny had kept the tickets in his wallet until that very morning without ever working up the courage to ask Tiffany to go with him. He had been too busy helping Sang Le with his English and working on the science project and worrying about exams. He had bought a heart-shaped box of chocolates for Tiffany, but chickened out at the last minute and gave it to his sisters.

"Man, what's the matter with you, Danny? You know Tiffany likes you. She always says hi to you and smiles that big, friendly smile." He grinned and put one hand on his waist and the other on his hair and pretended to be a girl wiggling her hips. A group of students in the hall laughed at him.

"It's not that, Cal. I've been too busy. Really. You know I've been helping my cousin. And I've been looking for a job for me and him, too."

"Ple-e-ease, give me a break. That's always your excuse. Look, I see her pretty little highness coming down the hall right now. I want you to turn your skinny butt around and ask her to the dance. If you don't, I'm going to burn our science project to the ground. I'm sick and tired of hearing you moping 'bout that girl."

Calvin slapped his hands onto Danny's shoulders and turned him toward the east hall. Tiffany was wearing a red dress and shoes with tiny heels. She had never looked so fine. Danny caught his breath.

"I can't, man," he finally said.

"Why not?"

"I sold those dance tickets this morning at the bus stop. To Tom Boggess."

"Tom Boggess! That guy couldn't get a date if he was covered with hundred-dollar bills. No, make that thousand-dollar bills. Why'd you do a crazy thing like that, Danny?"

"I knew I didn't have time for the dance. Besides, like I told you already, I have to be at the New Year's party my folks are having tonight."

"Right, you told me, but I didn't believe it. I didn't think anything was more important to you than a date with Tiffany Marie Schultz."

"You know I can't get out of it, Cal. It's a family tradition. It's like Christmas. I'm the oldest son, and I have to set a good example for the younger kids. There's lots of food. Why don't you come over? We eat about midnight."

"Food. Hmm, your mom is a great cook. I love those little baby egg rolls. Okay, I'll come. I'll bring the parts for the science project. Maybe we can work on it."

"Good. See if you can sleep over. We'll stay up all night and get that thing finished once and for all."

"All right! Now you're talking like the old Danny I used to know. We'll get an A on this thing yet." They slapped hands. "Too bad about the dance. I betcha Tiffany would have gone with you, too."

"Cal!" Danny cringed as his friends' words seemed to boom across the hall. Tiffany was standing less than ten feet away, next to her locker mate, her blue eyes focused directly on him. There was no way she could have missed Cal's loud mouth. All Danny could do was hide his face inside his locker.

"Hi, Danny." He heard her voice. Maybe it was his imagination, but Danny thought it quivered a little. He drew in a deep breath and forced himself to look up.

"Hi. Uh . . . I guess you heard what Calvin said."

She shrugged. "Not exactly. Something about the Valentine's Dance, wasn't it?" She opened her locker and stood back a minute while the other girl took out some books. Danny noticed Tiffany holding her history book.

"Did you get any studying done for the history test?" Danny asked, hoping a change of subject would clear the air.

She nodded. "Not as much as I wanted. There are a lot of things about the Vietnam War I don't understand. My dad was over there, but . . . well, he never talked about it much. I have a lot of questions—"

"Yeah, me, too," her locker mate quickly interrupted. "My uncle was over there and he said little kids would carry guns and bombs. He says the Vietcong would give little kids a candy bar for shooting Americans. Did you ever shoot anybody, Danny?"

Danny felt his face turn red and was speechless. He had never even seen an American until he was at the refugee camp in the Philippines in 1982. And that was the first time he'd even eaten a candy bar—a chocolate bar that he thought was the nastiest thing he'd ever tasted and spat out. As far as Vietcong, Danny didn't know what one was until he came to the United States.

"Ashley! You are so rude!" Tiffany's blue eyes flashed as she swung around and faced the girl. "Didn't you read your history book at all? The Vietnam War's been over for twenty years. Danny wasn't even born. Of course he never carried a gun. You are so ignorant." The other girl glared a moment, then stomped away.

"I'm sorry, Danny. Ashley can be so ignorant sometimes," Tiffany said breathlessly, her own face blotched with red.

Danny shrugged and forced a smile. "No sweat. I'm used to stuff like that. Hell, if she wants to think I ran around the jungle shooting M-16s and throwing hand grenades, who cares?" Danny shifted his weight and started to walk away, but Tiffany put her hand on his arm very gently, just enough to make him stop.

"I started to call you," she said softly.

Danny felt his lower jaw drop. "When?"

"Last night. I had some questions. I mean, about Vietnam and all. I wanted to, but . . ."

"I wish you had called."

"My brother Frank was on the phone most of the night. He's always hogging the phone when he's home. Which isn't very much anymore." She reached into her locker and idly fiddled with a fuzzy white cardigan for a moment. "Anyway, so I heard you bought tickets for the Valentine's Dance. I guess you're all ready for it and everything." She faced him then and leaned on the locker. Her eyes would not let him turn away. They pulled him like a cool blue tracking beam from the *Starship Enterprise*.

Danny swallowed hard. "Actually, I don't have any tickets. Not anymore. Something came up. A big family party tonight. It's Vietnamese New Year for the next three days. I wanted to go to the dance; I planned to ask you, but . . . well, my grandmother and parents are old-fashioned about all the family being home tonight. I don't suppose you would have wanted to go with me to the dance anyway, though."

A light burst into her eyes and Danny was sure he heard a tiny sigh escape from her lips. "Don't be silly. Of course I would have gone with you, Danny Vo. You're one of the neatest guys I know." She slammed the locker and smiled her biggest smile. "Here, Happy Valentine's Day." She handed him a big red envelope then dashed into the history classroom.

As Danny opened it and read the sweet lines of poetry, he felt like his heart was skipping every other beat and his face was on fire. He didn't feel real. He couldn't believe this was happening. Tiffany Marie Schultz, the most wonderful girl on the planet, liked him.

He wasn't sure how he survived first period. All Danny remembered was gazing at the back of Tiffany's head, at the way her soft blond hair spilled over the collar of her red dress. Every now and then someone would deliver flowers to a girl in the room. Each time, Tiffany would look up and follow the bouquet. Danny wanted to slap his head. Why hadn't he thought of sending her flowers?

Caught between self-adoration for being "neat" and self-hatred for not giving her anything, Danny stumbled through the history test and through the day. During lunch break, he dashed down the street to a convenience store to buy Tiffany a corsage or flowers or a heart-shaped box of candy. The store was sold out of the cheap ones and he didn't have enough money to buy the fancy ones, so he got an ugly card—all the pretty ones were gone. As the day progressed and more girls received candy and flowers, Danny felt more like a fool than ever. He couldn't find Tiffany, so he left the card taped to her locker.

By the end of the day Danny was tired, hungry from skipping lunch, and in the worst mood possible. His lighthearted feeling of wonder from that morning's encounter at the locker had turned into the deepest, darkest depression. He didn't even want to face Tiffany at her locker when the final bell of the day rang. Maybe she didn't want to see him, either, because she was not there, but the card was gone, so she must have found it.

While Danny's eyes searched the hallway, Sang Le trotted up to the locker, out of breath. His face was flushed.

"Cousin, cousin," he said as he tugged at Danny's sleeve. "Good news for you."

"Great, I need some good news."

"I look for you at lunchtime."

"I was busy."

Danny shoved his books inside the locker and jerked out his heavy coat that had been hanging on the hook since the last cold front. The weather had warmed up and he didn't think he would need it much longer.

"Beautiful girl want to talk to you."

"What?" Danny's eyes flew open.

"Over there, behind potted tree. She say she like you and want to date you. I invite her to our Tet celebration tonight."

"You what? Are you crazy? You asked Tiffany Marie Schultz to come to our apartment? No, man, our apartment is too ugly. I don't want her to see where I live."

Danny slammed his fist against the locker next to his. Sang Le's face registered a cloud of confusion.

"I no talk about American girl. I talk about beautiful rose—Hong. We have to ask her sister Cuc to come. And her uncle. It's only proper."

"Ask whoever you want, Sang Le. What's it got to do with me?"

"Hong say she like you. She want to date you, maybe marry."

"Marry! You're crazy! I don't want to marry Hong. I told you before, she's not my type. She's too old-fashioned. Can't you see I'm not interested in her? Now, leave me alone. I'm going home with Calvin. We're going to work on our science project. Tell my mother I'll be home in time to get ready for the party." Danny slammed the locker door and pivoted, not bothering to look at his cousin's face.

As Danny passed by the large potted tree, he

heard a sob. He saw Hong sitting on the floor, her hands over her face.

"Oh, shoot," Danny muttered, guessing that she had heard every word his big mouth had screamed. "Hong, I'm sorry," Danny said, but she leapt to her feet and ran away.

Danny saw his cousin running after her. Whether or not he reached her, Danny didn't know and didn't care. If he were a truly good person, he would humor his cousin and be nice to Hong. He would sacrifice his own feelings to keep harmony in the family. He wished he could be as generous as Sang Le, who was apparently willing to put aside his own feelings for Hong, to make her happy.

But Danny wasn't feeling generous at the moment. He was tired of always putting the family first. Bà would say Danny was being self-ish like a spoiled American. She would remind him again of how Sang Le had sacrificed every-thing to save Danny at the lotus moat ten years ago and would probably make him listen to the story again. She would say he wasn't behaving like a noble dragon-child, but he didn't care. He wasn't going to date Hong just to make Sang Le happy. This time Danny was going to put his own desires first and worry about the conse-quences later.

Chapter Seven

Late Friday evening, as Danny trudged up the stairs, what he wanted more than anything else was sleep. He had worked on his science project with Calvin, putting up with Lashandra's demands and the constant noise of Calvin's mother and her friends exercising to a Richard Simmons videotape. He had a splitting headache and couldn't wait to crash on his bed for a while before he dressed for the New Year's party. But what he got was a house full of noise.

Lan was waiting for him in front of the apartment door. Her bright blue *ao dai* contrasted nicely with the fluttering red streamers hanging on either side of the entry. Black characters that looked similar to Chinese writing covered each long, narrow strip of paper. Though Danny couldn't read the ancient Vietnamese form of writing, *chu nom,* he knew they were New Year's greetings.

"Danny, where have you been?" Lan asked, her arms folded and her face dark with worry.

"I was at Calvin's house working on our science project. I told Sang Le to give Má the message."

"Sang Le didn't come home from school. Má thought something must have happened to you and him on the bus. She's really worried."

Danny sighed heavily. His plans for a quick nap before the Tet festivities vanished. Now it looked like he would have to work extra hard to make it up to his mother for causing her anxiety.

Danny tossed his books onto his bed, then banged on the bathroom door to make Kim come out long enough for him to shower. With his freshly washed hair slicked back, Danny changed into new clothes—dressy black pants, a brilliant new white shirt, and a multicolored tie that almost blinded his eyes. Like everyone else in the family he walked about in his stocking feet.

The kitchen buzzed with activity as his aunts

and mother put the finishing touches on the midnight feast. In the corner, Bà hovered over the family altar arranging a bouquet of flowers, bright orange persimmons, a small round watermelon, and steaming bowls of rice. She lit the incense joss sticks and soon a sweet fragrance blended with the aroma of roasted duck that permeated every corner of the living room. But her pride and joy was the feeble stick of *hoa mai,* which had miraculously managed to produce three frail yellow blooms. The twig took the place of honor in the center of the dining table. The artificial tree that Danny's mother had paid so much money for had been relegated to the front porch to greet the New Year's visitors, who would be arriving soon after midnight.

At ten o'clock Kim stepped into the living room. Danny's mouth dropped when he saw the lovely pink silk *ao dai* that fit her trim figure like a glove. Somehow she had managed to hide the orange streak in her hair with a cluster of artificial pink peach blossoms. Under the long, snug tunic that opened on the sides, she wore billowy white silk pants. Even Bà, in her red *ao dai,* had been transformed from a bony old woman of sour disposition into a respectable elder full of patience and wisdom. She looked wise and kind as she bowed three times before the altar and pressed her hands together in prayer. Each family member followed her example, sending prayers to their ancestors for a safe journey to earth and praying for a healthy, prosperous new year.

Bà smiled at everyone and said the sweetest things about her grandchildren. Seated in her favorite chair, she called all the children to her. With great ceremony and wishes of a happy and healthy New Year, she handed each of the younger children a small, shiny red envelope. Each child bowed and thanked her, trying not to appear too eager when he or she tore open the *li-xi* and counted the money inside. Even though Bà didn't have to give money to the older children, she handed an envelope to Danny and to Sang Le, who had crept through the door only minutes before the ceremony began. Danny sighed with relief when he saw that his cousin was all right.

Sang Le stepped forward, carrying an awkward bundle wrapped in newspapers. He set it down gently in front of Bà. Her eyes twinkled as she removed the papers to reveal a large-as-life plaster-of-Paris dog—a black-and-white cocker spaniel.

Lan and Thuy broke into giggles. Even Bà chuckled as she turned it around, trying to determine what it was used for. Sang Le lifted the plaster dog and shook it. Loose change rattled in the bottom.

"It is a bank," Sang Le said in Vietnamese. "I am putting all the money I earn in here to repay all of you for bringing me to America. And for your new house, Bà."

"Oh, my precious grandson," Bà said. She threw her arms around Sang Le's neck. "Only you would think of such a thing."

"I am trying to find a good job," Sang Le added. "I will keep nothing for myself, except to buy school supplies. I don't want to be a burden on this family."

"You don't have to get a job," Danny's father quickly said. "We will take care of you while you are in school. You are equal to my own children. Study and get a good job. There will be time enough for repayments later."

Danny knew his father was sincere. He had told him the same thing many times. But Danny also had seen the pain in his father's eyes when his wife came home from working two jobs. Danny knew that despite his father's grand and generous offers, he would not mind if Danny or Sang Le got a job.

Sang Le must have understood, also, for he merely bowed and did not protest. He quietly distributed small presents wrapped in red tissue paper to Danny's younger brother and sisters, and to Uncle Dao's two small children. The gifts were small items that he had made in art class. The baby stuck her toy in her mouth and screamed with delight.

The children brought down the traditional *bau-ca-tom-cua* game, a lively gambling game that they played every New Year. Soon the house was filled with laughing and cheering.

The table was almost ready for the feast, and it was a few minutes until midnight, when the doorbell rang.

"Oh, perhaps that is Mr. Duy," Bà whispered. She shuffled all the children toward the front door, urging them to stand straight and lining them up in order of age. "The first guest is the most important. He will determine the luck for the rest of the year. You must show him the greatest respect," she instructed them.

Danny opened the door expecting to see the shriveled old face and white goatee of Mr. Duy.

"What's happening, man? Do I smell food?" Calvin Pickney stood in the doorway, his arms cradling a box of metal parts and electronic odds and ends.

No one said a word.

"Hey, aren't you going to let me in? It's

starting to get chilly out here." Calvin's dark brown eyes searched the shocked faces in front of him. Danny bit his lip to keep from laughing, but Bà's face was the color of her gray hair.

"No!" she shrieked in broken English. "You bad luck. Go away!" Her thin arms waved frantically at Calvin, then she grabbed a broom from the hall closet and swept at his feet. "I sweep away bad luck—go, go away, bad luck!" She kept sweeping at his feet until he was forced back on the staircase.

"I'm cool, I'm cool," Calvin said as he backed down the stairs. "I knew your grandma was crazy, Danny, but she's really weird this time."

Danny rushed after Bà, trying to take the broom from her. He was amazed at the strength in her frail arms.

"Bà, it's okay, it's okay. Calvin just came over to work on our science project." He explained as best he could in Vietnamese, though he had no idea how to convey the words "science" and "project," so he said them in English.

"No, he bring bad luck. Go home, bad spirit." She made catlike hissing noises at Calvin, who stood wide-eyed, his arms hugging the box. The air outside had grown cooler and now a soft mist steadily fell and beaded up in Calvin's curly hair.

"What do you want me to do, man?" Calvin called from the bottom of the stairs.

"Stay there, Cal. If you come in now, she'll blame you for every single bad thing that happens to this family this year. Just hold on a few minutes until Mr. Duy gets here."

While Danny tried to keep Bà from going down the stairs with the broom, he saw an old man shuffling slowly down the sidewalk. His black French beret and expensive but worn French jacket looked oddly out of place on his slender old form. In spite of his umbrella, a layer of mist covered the red cellophone of the fruit basket and the dark green bottle of Remy Martin cognac in his hands. He paused at the bottom of the stairs, nodded to Calvin, then started up.

"Uh-hum," Calvin cleared his throat. "Is this who you were expecting, Grandma?" he asked.

Bà stopped fussing and looked down. She dropped the broom immediately. "Oh, Mr. Duy. *Cung chuc Tan Xuan.*" She greeted him with the formal New Year's greeting and motioned for him to climb up the stairs. "We are so happy you honor us by being our first visitor of the New Year. May you have a long and happy life."

"Chuc mung nam moi," he replied as he tipped his beret and bowed from the waist. "And a healthy, prosperous New Year to you and your

family, Madame Truong." His English had a strong French accent, for he had lived most of his life in Saigon.

Danny hurried down the stairs and took the box from Calvin's arms.

"Sorry about that," he whispered. "I swear she gets more crazy every year. Let's just wait here a few minutes until Mr. Duy's safely inside."

"I don't know, man." Calvin shook his head. "Does she really think I'm a bad spirit?"

Danny pulled Calvin up the stairs by his jacket sleeve.

"Forget about it. Once the eating starts, nobody will notice you. A lot more people will be coming in a few minutes. We'll be popping firecrackers at midnight."

"Isn't that against the law? It's not even the Fourth of July."

While they talked on the patio, Uncle Dao stepped out, followed by the younger children and Sang Le. Uncle Dao held a string of red firecrackers in one hand and lit it with his cigarette lighter.

"He's crazy, man," Calvin shouted as a roar erupted in the night like machine-gun fire and bits of red paper spewed everywhere. "He could lose his fingers that way."

"Ah, these little firecrackers nothing," Dao

said with a grin. "We do it all the time in Vietnam." He handed a bundle of firecrackers to Sang Le, who tied it onto the end of a stick and lit it for Dao's little boy. The girls put their fingers in their ears and the baby screamed in terror.

A few seconds later, they heard the muffled thunder of more firecrackers from across the apartment courtyard and then down by the abandoned swimming pool. Someone's car alarm went off and added annoying honks and beeps to the racket.

"Ha! The Tran family," Uncle Dao shouted. "We beat them this year." He scooped up the baby and wiped her tears and kissed her creamy smooth cheeks. "Evil spirits won't come to this house," he said to her. "The loud noise scared them away."

A few minutes later a family dressed in finery paraded across the courtyard and tromped up the stairs. Each one greeted Uncle Dao and Danny and Bà with a bow and the traditional wish for long life, health, and prosperity during the coming year. Within ten minutes two more families arrived.

Bà greeted each new guest graciously, then leaned the broom against the porch rail. She would use it again on the last day of Tet to sweep the red firecracker debris into the house, a way of collecting good fortune during the coming year.

Inside, the dining table was covered with food. The children still played their gambling games, and some of the men sat in a circle on the floor and started a game of *sap sam,* a version of poker using thirteen cards.

By the time the last of the guests had arrived, the small apartment was bursting at the seams and spilling out onto the spacious concrete landing.

"Where are we going to work on our project?" Calvin asked as he munched on a crispy shrimp chip. He tried to dip a piece of roasted duck into brown sauce with his chopsticks, but it landed in his lap.

"In my room tonight," Danny said. "In the morning we can go out on the patio to do the painting and gluing."

After eating, Danny and Calvin closed the bedroom door and spread the pieces of the miniature house out on the bed. They tried to concentrate on the work, but it was hopeless. Most of the men were shouting and laughing in the animated card game. Other men were making up clever verses of poetry, each one trying to outwit the previous poet. Children were squealing and shouting and running down the hall, constantly bumping against the wall. Danny jerked the door open and looked down at five small faces. From the kitchen he heard his grandmother complaining in a high-pitched, irritating voice.

"What's all the noise about?" he asked his little brother.

"Bà cut the watermelon open and it was rotten in the middle. She says it means the worst luck ever in the coming year."

"Oh, for . . ." Danny slammed the door and mumbled under his breath. "I swear that old woman and her superstitions are going to drive me crazy, Cal. She's gone berserk because the New Year's watermelon isn't red all the way through." He shook his head and crawled back onto the bed.

"Watermelon in February? That doesn't seem natural. But as long as she doesn't blame me for it, I don't care," Calvin said. He plugged in a soldering iron and removed a piece of metal from the box. Before long the sharp, suffocating odor of hot iron and melting solder filled the room. A soft rap on the door interrupted their work.

"Come in, Sang Le," Danny said as he opened the door. "Sorry about all the mess. We'll have it cleaned up in a little while. Guess you're ready to go to bed, huh?"

"No, no. I'm still awake. I just got tired of answering so many questions from everyone," he said in Vietnamese. He glanced at Calvin's curious face, then smiled. "Sorry, I speak Vietnamese, Calvin; English no good. Too many question in there." He nodded toward the rest of the apartment.

"Yeah? What kind of questions?" Cal asked.

"My head hurt from too much question. About communists; about Hong Kong; about jail."

"About what?" Calvin cocked his head to one side.

"Jail," Sang Le repeated the word three more times, but Calvin still didn't understand.

"Jail, prison," Danny finally interrupted.

"English too hard," Sang Le said as he plopped onto the floor and lit up a cigarette, a habit he had acquired as a boy. "Americans never understand me; teachers never understand me. Maybe I quit school."

"Hey, don't give up," Calvin said as he slapped Sang Le's shoulder. "You're learning."

Sang Le nodded and puffed, then glanced at the boxes and the mess on the floor. "What you do?"

After Danny and Calvin explained that they were trying to build a house, Sang Le quickly picked up a pair of tin snips and a thin sheet of metal.

"I help," he said eagerly.

"Dan-*ny*," Calvin whispered between tightly closed lips and sat on the edge of the bed. "This is one-third of our science grade, remember?"

Danny waved Calvin back and shook his head as he watched his cousin drawing something with soapstone onto the tin.

"What's that?" Calvin asked.

"It's *chim-phuong-hoang*. It bring your little science house very good luck."

"What's a *chim fung* . . . whatever you said?"

"It's something like a phoenix," Danny explained. "A bird that's supposed to bring good luck and happiness. Look, Sang Le, you don't have to go to that much trouble. It's supposed to be an American house, anyway. You really don't have to . . ."

But Sang Le was too deeply immersed in his project now. He began cutting tiny pieces of a design that only his eyes could see.

"Don't worry," Danny whispered to Calvin as he pulled him into the hallway out of earshot, "I'll buy another piece of tin if this one gets messed up. I can't tell him no. This is the first time I've seen him look happy in two weeks. School has really been getting him down. Learning English is a lot harder than he expected. And he can't keep up with the other classes if he doesn't understand what the teachers are saying. Let's just leave him alone a few minutes."

Danny and Calvin returned to the kitchen and feasted some more, this time on shrimp and cucumber salad and the traditional *banh chung* and *banh giay* New Year's cakes. Calvin made faces as he bit into the gooey rice with pieces of pork hidden in the middle, and he refused to even taste the squid. He made comments about the spongy-looking ground pork cake and almost spat out the spicy strips of sweetened ginger root. He challenged Lan and two little girls to a game using fried watermelon seeds but lost miserably.

When they returned to the bedroom, Sang Le was still squatting on his heels over the pieces of tin that he was busily soldering together. The acrid smell of melting solder almost knocked Danny and Calvin off their feet when they opened the door. They waved at the smoky fumes and coughed. Danny opened the window and tried to fan some of the bad air out. Sang Le did not seem to notice. The smoke from the cigarette dangling from the corner of his mouth must have covered up the other odors. Even though it was cool outside, he had removed his shirt. Beads of sweat rolled down his temples and down his bare back covered with long, thin scars. Danny swallowed hard. He didn't have to use too much imagination to figure out how the scars had gotten there.

Danny and Calvin worked on their project until about three in the morning, but sleep overtook them both and they crashed on the bed fully clothed. Danny heard the phone ring once and through a groggy veil of sleep heard Sang Le speaking soft Vietnamese. He heard the names Cuc and Hong and formed a mental picture of the last time he had seen Hong. He remembered her sad, weeping face as she had sat on the hallway floor behind the potted tree earlier that day. He groaned slightly in his sleep, then rolled over.

The next time Danny woke up, it was six-thirty and the house was quiet. Calvin was snoring, his body half off the bed, his arms wrapped around his pillow. Danny felt a cool draft and heard a noise at the window. Sang Le was climbing through it.

"What happened?" Danny asked in a husky voice, rubbing his eyes.

"Nothing, cousin," Sang Le replied in Vietnamese.

Danny smelled beer and thought his cousin's words sounded slurred. "Where have you been?"

"I went for a walk."

"At six-thirty in the morning?"

Sang Le shrugged. "I had some thinking to do. I met a friend."

"A friend? Hey, I didn't know you had any friends yet. Anybody I know?"

"No. He was in the refugee camp in Hong Kong, too. Not at the same time as me. He came to America three years ago. His name is Tho."

"Well, get some sleep. You know Bà has all kinds of stuff planned for today. We're supposed to watch the lion dance downtown at ten o'clock."

Sang Le nodded. His bunk bed was occupied by a small boy, so he lay on the floor.

"You can have my place on the bed," Danny offered, but his cousin refused.

"I am used to the hard floor. I like it better than the soft mattress."

Danny closed his eyes, but he could not go back to sleep. He lay on his back, perfectly still, waiting for what he knew would come next. A few moments later he heard the familiar sound of his cousin crying out in his sleep, whimpering and sometimes screaming.

Knowing sleep was gone from him, Danny

stood up and flipped on the desk lamp. Its pale glow landed on something shiny on the floor. Danny leaned over and saw the shimmering metal phoenix. Each feather in its long, flowing tail had been cut out separately and painted in every color of the rainbow. The miniature house had been completed, and the bird gracefully perched on the roof.

"Wow," Danny whispered and glanced at his sleeping cousin. "Thanks, Sang Le," he said softly. His cousin whimpered in reply.

Three hours later Danny dragged Calvin out of bed.

"We've got an A in the bag," Calvin said when he saw the completed house with the unique phoenix on its roof. He exchanged high-fives with Danny and Sang Le.

Danny, Calvin, and Sang Le rode with Aunt Lien downtown where Uncle Dao was already waiting, carefully hanging fifty-foot strings of red firecrackers from the roof of his video store.

A pickup had already arrived loaded with colorfully costumed kung fu students, musical instruments, and a giant artificial lion for the parade.

"That's a funny-looking lion," Calvin said.

"It's really a *ky-lan,* part dog and part lion,"

Sang Le explained as the huge red-and-gold-and-green "lion" strutted from side to side in rhythm to pounding drums, gongs, and clanking cymbals, and firecrackers exploding at their feet. It danced and rolled over and skillfully ate money-stuffed cabbages dangling from the shop roofs. It winked its big eyes at the crowd.

In a roped-off section of the street, local kung fu schools demonstrated their skills. The sun was shining brightly and the air was crisp. Everyone was laughing and happy except for Sang Le. He stared at his own shadow, oblivious to the throng around him.

"What's wrong, cousin?" Danny shouted as the first twenty-foot string of red firecrackers popped on the nearest restaurant roof. He stuck a finger in his ear and wiggled it to help restore his hearing during a pause in the noise.

"The *ma qui*—shadow spirits—are out to-day," Sang Le replied in his native tongue.

"That's good, isn't it?" Danny asked.

Sang Le shook his head slowly. "No, hasn't Bà told you about the *ma qui*? All people have goodness and evil in them. Our bad spirits, the things that make us do wrong, live in our shadows. They follow us everywhere bringing bad luck and sadness. In Vietnam, if you have done bad things all year or have had really bad luck, you can destroy the *ma qui* by destroying your shadow."

Danny crinkled his brow. "How do you kill a shadow?"

"With great difficulty, little cousin. You must put it in great danger—stand in the path of a car, a train, a charging water buffalo."

"Isn't that kind of risky?"

"Oh yes, sometimes the unfortunate person is killed along with his shadow. But at least the evil spirits die with him. Sometimes that is the only way to get rid of them. It is worth the risk. A life with bad spirits is worse than being dead."

Danny moved his arm and watched the dark shadow move with him. Suddenly he felt a shiver and had the urge to run from it.

"Hey, you two, speak English once in a while, will ya," Calvin said impatiently. "What are you blabbering about anyway?"

"You wouldn't believe it if I told you," Danny muttered. "And I don't think you want to know."

"I thought you said all Vietnamese are supposed to be happy today." Calvin turned to Sang Le. "Doesn't all this make you think about New Year's in Vietnam?"

Sang Le nodded. "Yes, I think about Vietnam. I think about my mother and last time I see her nine year ago. She have no money for *banh chung*. She save pennies and buy me five firecracker. I very happy. I feel like king that day. But it nothing like this." Sang Le waved his hand toward the bustling street filled with laughing, cheerful people.

Suddenly he switched to rapid Vietnamese, forgetting that Calvin could not understand. "In re-education camp we received one small piece of pork in our ration of rice on the first day of Tet. That was the only way we knew the New Year had arrived. In Hong Kong, I had nothing at all. Now I see all of this and I feel sad."

An uneasy feeling crept over Danny as he watched his cousin's eyes stare blankly into the distance.

"There is so much wealth here, Duong," Sang Le continued. "I am happy for you and for everyone who came to America, yet I cannot forget those who are still in my homeland."

Danny nodded, though in his heart he wasn't sure he understood what his cousin meant. He started to ask a question, but the sight of a familiar black jacket with the yellow cobra made the words freeze in his throat. He should have known Cobra would be here. He would be celebrating the New Year like everyone else. Danny's eyes followed the small, wiry man as he picked his way through the crowd, often completely buried from sight by the taller people around him. Danny expected to see the crowd part, as the grass parts when a serpent crawls through it, but no one else seemed to notice the sinister black eyes and chiseled features.

Suddenly Cobra stopped. He stared right at Danny. He nodded, then walked toward them. Cobra's chubby friend waved at Danny, grinning, and shouted something obscene about his "ugly sisters." But when he and his other two friends started to follow Cobra, their leader waved them back and walked alone. He looked like a tiny ant separated from its co-workers, weaving right and left to avoid people.

"Come on, let's go to the other side of the street," Danny said. "We can see the kung fu better from over there."

"No, man, those firecrackers have just about busted my eardrums open," Calvin protested. "I don't want to get any closer."

Danny tried to lead Calvin and Sang Le by their arms, but they both resisted.

"Chao anh, mung xuan moi." He heard the familiar voice of Cobra and knew it was too late. When Danny turned, he was surprised to see that Cobra was not even talking to him. He was addressing Sang Le.

"And Happy New Year, good health, and prosperity to you, too, Tho," Sang Le replied with a slight bow.

"Tho?" Danny's voice registered the shock.

"Cousin Duong, this is Nguyen Van Tho, the friend I told you about. I met him near the Queen Bee club the night we found Kim. He is the one who was in the Hong Kong refugee camp just before I was there. Tho, this is my little cousin Duong and his friend Calvin."

"As American say, small world," Cobra said in choppy English as his black eyes stared at Danny. He seemed almost amused at the coincidence, and the corners of his thick lips turned up slightly.

Danny wanted to groan. And to think that he had been happy that Sang Le had finally made a friend. Danny was speechless, but Cobra didn't seem to notice. He turned to the lion dance and the kung fu performers and the happy faces in the crowd.

"All day long all I think about is Vietnam," Cobra said softly to the air. "I have no one left there who cares about me, yet I miss it. I look at all this and think, so much wealth and happiness here and so much sadness and poverty in my homeland. I feel guilty to celebrate. Do you understand?"

"Yes," Sang Le quickly replied and his eyes

lit up. "I was just telling my cousin the same thing."

"A true son or daughter of Vietnam cannot help but think of our motherland today," Cobra said. His cold black eyes glowed as they peered into Danny's face. Suddenly his voice turned bitter. "*You* don't understand, do you? You are an *American,* not Vietnamese."

Danny shifted his weight. He shoved his hands into his jeans pockets and glanced at Calvin. He didn't want to embarrass his friend with talk about homelands and corny stuff like that, but he couldn't stand Cobra's tone of voice. "I know what it feels like to be Vietnamese," Danny protested.

"Ha! Do you know what it means to suffer, to sacrifice?" His lips turned down and the words spewed out as bitter as gall. "Do you know what it is like to be the one left behind while the rest of your family lives in wealth in America? While you beg for food on the street and sleep with rats, your cousins and aunts and uncles wallow in American greed. No, you don't understand. But your cousin does. Don't you, friend? He wears the scars of the re-education camp, if not on his back or the bottoms of his feet, then in his heart." Cobra laid a small, delicate hand on Sang Le's shoulder.

Danny saw the look in his cousin's eyes as

he slowly nodded. Danny had seen the same look before in the eyes of children listening to an idolized older brother.

"Come with me to play *bida* and to eat at a good Vietnamese restaurant I know," Cobra said to Sang Le. "We will talk about Vietnam and real Vietnamese people who still live there. Leave these pampered *Americans* to their hamburgers and Coca-Colas. I will wait for you across the street."

"Sang Le, don't go with him." Danny grabbed his cousin's jacket sleeve as he started to follow Cobra.

"No, Duong, I must go with my friend. I will join you later."

"We're supposed to ride with Uncle Dao over to the Distinguished Vietnamese Citizens Center right after the lion dance. Thuy has to recite his poem and Lan is in the folk dance. And Aunt Lien is singing some old-fashioned songs. She's a terrific singer, you've got to hear her. And they'll be playing those old-fashioned instruments you like so much—the little guitar and that zither thing."

"*Ty ba* and *dan tranh*."

"Yeah, if you say so. And flutes and lots of electric guitars and pretty women and good-looking girls singing and dancing. And the men banging the drums and the gongs in front of the altar. You'll love it. Oh, and tons of food and a dragon dance and more firecrackers. You've got to come. Bà will be brokenhearted if you don't."

Danny's cousin stared at Cobra standing across the street, calmly smoking a cigarette. With all the self-assurance of a prince, he didn't even bother to look their way. Sang Le heaved a long, heavy sigh.

"I would love to attend the ceremony, but I must go with Tho. Right now he needs a friend more than Bà needs a grandson."

"A friend!" Danny exclaimed in disbelief. "You don't know about Tho. He's—" Danny glanced around to make sure none of Cobra's friends were near. "He's *du dang*—a gang leader. They call him Cobra. Man, he's just a punky hoodlum."

"No, you are wrong. He is my *friend*." Sang Le brushed past Danny and squeezed through the crowd as he crossed the street.

Danny and Calvin watched him until he had vanished into the throng of laughing, happy people.

"What was all *that* about, Dan-o?" Calvin asked.

"Sorry we were speaking Vietnamese again, Cal. That guy doesn't speak English very well."

"He's in a gang, isn't he?"

"I think so. His friends call him Cobra."

"That suits his scaly face and little beady eyes. What were you arguing about?"

"Sang Le is going with Cobra to play billiards instead of coming with us. Bà is going to be mad."

"Are you going after him?"

"I don't know," Danny replied. "I suppose it's none of my business what he does."

"Man, that Cobra guy gives me the shivers."

"I know what you mean." Danny saw the martial arts demonstration breaking up and his Uncle Dao waving for them to come to the car. "I guess I won't go after my cousin this time, but I can tell you one thing: if Sang Le gets involved with Cobra, he would probably be a lot better off if he had stayed in Vietnam and slept with the rats."

Chapter Eight

The misty dragon's breath of February turned into the billowy winds of March without event. Bà tilled the soil in a flower bed near the abandoned pool and planted her garden of onions, cilantro, Chinese radishes, mint, and lemon grass. Her bitter melon vine had already established itself at the foot of the concrete stairs. By the end of the summer it would coil over the rails and poke its vivid green leaves onto the rooftop, letting its crinkled cucumber-sized orbs dangle over the concrete landing.

Danny marked the days off on his calendar one by one as time crept toward his "official" sixteenth birthday. He practiced his parallel parking and taught his cousin to drive, too. Though Sang Le had turned eighteen and drove with the eye and hand of an expert, he could not pass the written test. He memorized the multiple choice answers on Danny's test, but the exams kept changing. After the third time, he refused to go back, saying he would take his chances and drive without a license, if ever he had the luck to own a car. But first he had to find a job.

Danny knew exactly how his cousin felt. So many of his hopes and dreams seemed to rely on finding a job, too—any job. But the part of town he lived in had none of the normal sources for sixteen year olds—no movie houses, no fast-food restaurants. So, when Danny saw the "Help Wanted" sign in Tilson's Grocery Store, a small brick building that had been there since the 1960s, Danny did not hesitate to grab his cousin and hurry to the back of the store where Mr. Tilson was watching a produce truck back up to his loading dock.

Danny watched the plump man lean against the alley wall, take a long draw on his stubby cigar, and slowly exhale.

"I'm sorry, son," he said, shaking his head. "I'd like to hire you, but I can't." A trail of cigar ashes spilled to the pavement as the heavy man wiped a shirtsleeve across his damp forehead. He turned and barked orders to the driver of the truck. As the tailgate lowered, the sweet aroma of fruit drifted into the alley and blended with the smell of last week's rotting vegetables in the dumpster.

"But you have a 'Help Wanted' sign out front," Danny protested. Mr. Tilson was the uncle of a boy he knew at school, Jason Tilson. His was the only small privately owned grocery store in the neighborhood. Danny visited often to play video games. And he always bought something and never caused any trouble. Mr. Tilson had always acted friendly, but at the moment all of that didn't seem to matter.

"You're not old enough. I can tell that. What are you, thirteen or fourteen?"

"I'm the same age as your nephew, Jason—fifteen. I'll be sixteen in two weeks," Danny replied and straightened his back so he would look taller. He glanced at Sang Le, who stood by, his hands hanging at his sides as he tried to follow the conversation. His English was still choppy at best. Even though he could read a little, he could not follow the rapid speech patterns of native speakers of English.

The stocky man squinted at Danny from under thick eyebrows, chewing on his extinguished cigar.

"Fifteen ain't old enough," he replied. "The

law says you have to be sixteen. You don't want me breaking the law, do ya? I already got into trouble with the Labor Board once and don't want that to happen again." The pudgy man hoisted his low-slung belt over his bulging belly. As he stooped to lift a crate of tomatoes, the pants slipped back down, showing the top of his underwear. He grunted from the heavy load.

"But you let Jason work for you last summer," Danny gently reminded him.

"Well, he's my nephew. The law lets your own kin work for you even if they're under sixteen." He started to walk toward the back door of the store.

"Then give my cousin Sang Le the job. He's eighteen. He's strong, too. He'll do any kind of work." Danny whispered a few words of Vietnamese to his cousin. Sang Le nodded, then eagerly rushed to the grocer and slipped his hands under the crate of tomatoes. His arms knotted into small, hard muscles and his thin legs bent slightly as he carried the heavy load into the store.

"Is that the cousin who was in prison in Vietnam? He shot somebody, didn't he?" He turned to Sang Le. "I heard you were a Vietcong?"

"Vietcong?" Sang Le's face turned vivid. "No, no! I not communist!" He turned his head aside and spat.

Danny felt his face turn hot even though the spring air was pleasantly mild that Saturday morning. He was tired of having to tell older Americans that his family had nothing to do with the Vietcong—the communist guerrillas who fought in the southern part of Vietnam against the Americans. Even the Vietcong, mostly simple rice farmers, had to take a back seat to the northern communists after they conquered the south. And of course, all that happened before Sang Le was even born.

"Who said my cousin was in prison? Who said he was a Vietcong?" Danny clenched his fist behind his back and tried to speak calmly.

Mr. Tilson shrugged. "Don't remember. Some other teenagers who were in here looking for work."

"Well, my cousin wasn't in prison, Mr. Tilson, and he wasn't a communist. It was the communists who held him in re-education camp. That's like a political prison. They put people there who helped Americans during the war. People who risked their lives to help relatives get out after the Americans left."

"That so? Shoot, he must have been a little kid. What did he do to make the Commies so mad at a kid?"

Danny fought back his anger. He didn't want to open his family's affairs to outsiders. It was nobody's business, especially Mr. Tilson's. But Sang Le desperately wanted a job.

"My cousin said some things to the government soldiers when they brought the news that his father had died in re-education camp. He got mad and hit one of the officials." Danny decided he was not going to tell all the truth. It had really been Sang Le's mother who had gone mad and cursed and swung at the soldiers. Sang Le had been sent to re-education camp for trying to stop the soldiers from beating his mother.

"How many days did he get for that?"

"Years, Mr. Tilson. My cousin worked in a re-education camp doing hard labor for five years before he was released."

"Five years!" The grocer's eyes widened and he chomped down on the damp cigar. "I can't believe they'd do that to a kid."

"Sang Le was nine years old when he went to the Long Binh camp. A year after he was released, he escaped by boat to a refugee camp in Hong Kong. That's where he has been for the past two years."

"Well now, I am sorry to hear that, Danny." Mr. Tilson's voice and pudgy face softened for a moment. "He's had some kind of rough life, I suppose. Well, war is hell. Especially that mess in 'Nam." A long silence filled the air. Mr. Tilson shook his head and watched Sang Le lifting crates of vegetables and neatly stacking them near the bins inside the store. Finally the man pushed off the brick wall and tossed the cigar butt to the street.

"That's enough, son," he shouted to Sang Le and waved him over. "I can see you're a hard worker. Do you have a green card?"

Sang Le's questioning eyes darted from Mr. Tilson to Danny.

"Green card?" Mr. Tilson repeated.

Sang Le swallowed hard and glanced at his cousin.

"Sure, he's got a green card—"

"No, no, let him speak. Do you have a green card?"

"I work hard," Sang Le finally said, then rushed to the truck and grabbed another crate. Mr. Tilson cocked his head to one side and glanced at Danny.

"He doesn't understand English, does he?"

Danny felt as if someone had just kicked him in the stomach. He started to lie, then hung his head and stared at the filthy alley strewn with bits of packing straw.

"Well, not everything. But he's been enrolled in ESL class for almost two months now. He'll be speaking great with a little more practice."

Sang Le did not pause, even though beads of sweat slid down his temples and a wet spot showed through the back of his shirt. His large dark eyes darted from the grocer to Danny as he walked by, sensing that something was wrong. He watched Mr. Tilson's lips move, as if he could will himself to understand the foreign words coming out.

"Sorry, Danny," Mr. Tilson finally said. "I've had three other teenagers asking about this job. I need somebody who can speak English and handle the cash register when I'm busy in the back. I need somebody who can read the labels so he can stock goods. Darn, I wish that Culpepper boy wasn't so dumb-acting."

"Which Culpepper boy?"

"Well, actually—both of them applied for the job. One came last night and the other one early this morning. I know neither one is too bright, but . . ."

"Mike is really slow, Mr. Tilson. And lazy. And his brother Benny steals."

Danny felt awful about squealing on the Culpepper brothers. But he had no doubt that they were the ones who had told Mr. Tilson that Sang Le had been in prison. Under normal circumstances, Danny would keep anything he knew about someone to himself. He hesitated, glanced at his cousin's eager face, and recalled their conversation the night before. Sang Le would do anything at any price. But he didn't even want the money for himself. It was for Bà and for Danny's parents, so they could buy a house. Danny took a deep breath.

"I saw Benny stealing candy bars from the Stop-N-Go."

"Is that so?" Mr. Tilson arched an eyebrow.

"You don't want to hire him, Mr. Tilson."

"Well, maybe not, but he *does* speak English." The chubby grocer stepped over to Sang Le, who was lifting the last crate from the truck. The grocer laid a hand on Sang Le's shoulder. His fingers were as short and stubby as his cigar.

"Tell him to stop, Danny," he said. "No need for him to try to impress me anymore."

Danny spoke in Vietnamese to his cousin. Sang Le ignored the instructions and quickened his step until he had stacked the last crate inside the store. He spoke to Danny in Vietnamese as he walked back. They argued a moment, then Sang Le turned to Mr. Tilson.

"I work half pay." He pronounced the "p" like an "f." Mr. Tilson crinkled up his nose.

"Sorry, I didn't catch that."

"Mr. Tilson," Danny cleared his throat and shifted his weight, "my cousin says he'll work for half pay until he learns to speak English. He's a good worker. He may look skinny, but he's really strong and has more endurance than I do. He's used to hard work."

"I'd like to help him out, Danny, but it's the law. I have to pay minimum wage or I'll get busted by the government. That's what happened to me once already and they're still on my case about it. The IRS and Labor Board watch me like a bug under a microscope. Explain that to your cousin. Tell him to come back when he speaks English and I'll be glad to give him a chance. And *you* check back with me in two weeks when you're sixteen. Why don't you try some of those Chinese stores over on Bellaire Boulevard? They don't pay any attention to the law, anyhow." He bit the end off a fresh cigar and struck a match. A puff of smoke fouled the air.

Danny swallowed his anger and pulled Sang Le out of the alley into the sunlit street. Fat chance the job would still be there in two weeks. A gust of wind hit him in the face and he zipped up his windbreaker.

"Did you tell him I would work for half pay, little cousin?" Sang Le asked in rapid-fire Vietnamese. Danny had to concentrate to follow the words spilling from his cousin's lips.

"Yes, yes, I told him. But that's against the law here in America."

"American laws are crazy. In Vietnam anybody works at anything they can. Nobody cares how old you are. Everybody is glad to have any job they can get. Americans are spoiled." The corners of his lips turned down. It was a gesture that Danny had seen more and more over the past few weeks.

Sang Le quickened his pace and walked down the street, his hands shoved into the thin secondhand jacket that Bà had bought at a garage sale.

"Sang Le, wait up!" Danny shouted and trotted after the lean boy. In two months time, his cousin had gained hardly any weight at all. He was still thin and harried-looking. He always skipped lunch at school. Whether it was because he hated American food or because he was trying to save every penny, Danny wasn't sure.

"Don't worry, Sang Le. We'll find jobs. Uncle Dao said we could work for him at his video store downtown, as a last resort."

"We need cars to get downtown," Sang Le grumbled, his eyes staring straight ahead. "I don't have a car. You don't have a car. How can we get there? Maybe I can ride Thuy's bicycle."

"No, man, that's crazy. You're too old to be

riding a little bike like that. Besides, it's too far. It would take you two hours to get downtown from here."

"Too far? In Vietnam everybody rides a bicycle. Nobody drives cars but the greedy government pigs."

"Well, in case you haven't noticed lately, cousin, this isn't Vietnam. Maybe you could ride the bus to work. Or ride with Aunt Lien on weekends. We'll work something out. Hey, there's a bus. Let's go downtown now and check it out."

Both boys broke into a run as the red-white-and-blue Metro bus hissed to a stop in front of them. Since it was Saturday, the bus was almost empty. They took a seat near the back and stretched out.

Sang Le remained silent, deep in his own thoughts. Danny hated it when his cousin turned inward like that. And he had been doing it more and more lately. At first, Sang Le had put on a courageous front, always smiling his huge grin and nodding and laughing at his own blunders when he stumbled over English or didn't understand an American custom. But lately he didn't want to talk to Americans much. He only said a few words to Calvin now and then. The rest of the time he walked the school halls alone, or in the company of Hong and Cuc, who were not exactly sociable themselves.

"Sang Le," Danny broke the silence, "is Hong still mad at me?" He knew that if Sang Le would talk about anything, it would be Hong. He worshipped her, even if she didn't seem to return the affection.

Sang Le shrugged. "She doesn't tell me everything," he said in Vietnamese.

"Speak English, cousin." Danny gently prodded Sang Le's elbow. "You need the practice, don't you?"

"I don't care about English anymore," he said, still in his native tongue. "That ESL teacher is not fair. She speaks Spanish all the time when somebody else doesn't understand. But she never explains in Vietnamese when Hong or Cuc or I don't understand. How can I learn if she doesn't help me? If it weren't for Hong and Cuc, I wouldn't know anything. I don't understand this paper." He removed a white slip from his jacket pocket and handed it to Danny. "Cuc tried to explain it to me."

"Oh, yeah, report card time. I got mine yesterday, too. I haven't shown it to Má yet. She's going to scream when she sees my history grade. I hate history. Who wants to study about a bunch of old dead people? At least I made an A in physics, thanks to the science project." Danny slumped down lower in the bus seat and propped his feet up on the frame in front of him. He opened his cousin's report card and looked at the grades.

"Whew!" he half whistled. "That's pretty bad, cousin." Danny shook his head and chuckled. "As a matter of fact, that's about the worst report card I've ever seen. No wonder you're in such a bad mood. All Fs and Ds except for a C in P.E. And what's this—an A in art class? Who has to sign it? Bà? My mother? My father? Who's your official guardian?"

Sang Le drew in air, held it a long time, then let it out slowly. He took the card back and stared at it a long time. "Bà is my official sponsor. Do you think she will be angry? Is this 'report card' important?"

Danny threw his head back and laughed aloud. "I guess you could say that. Just your whole future depends on what kind of grades you make in high school. Especially if you want to get into college."

"College? I don't care about college. I don't care about high school. I just want a job. I will work at anything. Why is it so hard? The sign says 'help wanted' but that man didn't want a hard worker like me. In Vietnam we're glad for any work. Any work! Americans don't know how lucky they are to have some choices. Americans don't appreciate freedom of choice. You can never understand until you have lived under the thumb of the communists."

"Here we go again." Danny sighed and prepared to hear his cousin repeat his long dissertation about Americans' lack of gratitude.

He was almost asleep when the bus squealed to a stop at the corner of St. Emmanuel and Chartres streets on the edge of Chinatown. Danny and Sang Le jumped to their feet and darted out of the bus. At last his cousin stopped talking.

They walked along the sidewalks lined with Asian stores and restaurants. A hundred aromas filled the air: smoke from burnt won-tons, barbecue from ducks hanging upside down in a market window, sandalwood incense from an import store. The rich aroma of chicken and pork from the nearest restaurant reminded Danny that he hadn't eaten lunch yet. He hoped his aunt would have some food in their shop. Usually she walked next door to a combination French bakery/sandwich shop or down the block to a restaurant that specialized in *pho,* a soup with noodles, beef, and vegetables. Danny would have liked pizza, but he knew there was no way his cousin would consent to eating anything with cheese on it. Besides, Danny only had five dollars in his wallet and doubted that Sang Le had even that much. Lucky for them, Vietnamese food was abundant and cheap in this part of town.

A few American tourists wandered aimlessly in and out of shops, but otherwise everyone on the street was Asian—mostly Chinese and Vietnamese. Several of the shops had both languages written on the windows.

As soon as they had stepped off the bus, Sang Le's spirits rose. When he smelled the pungent air, he smiled.

"It reminds me of Vietnam," he said as he breathed deeply. "I miss my country so much. Sometimes I think I should have stayed. But a man released from re-education camp has no future. I could not go to school or get a job. In the future, even my children would not be allowed to enter a university." Suddenly he stopped. "Look, there is a *bida* place up ahead."

"No, Sang Le, you spend too much time playing billiards."

"Just one game, little cousin. One beer and one cigarette to help me relax before we speak to Uncle Dao about a job."

Danny grumbled under his breath, but followed Sang Le to the run-down billiards hall on the corner. As they stepped through the open door, thick cigarette smoke stung Danny's eyes. Clouds of smoke hovered over each billiard table where men were engaged in lively arguments and laughter. Everyone paused to stare at Danny and Sang Le as they walked in.

The owner, a friend of Uncle Dao, hurried over and welcomed them. Sang Le lit up a cigarette and took a cue stick. Soon he found an opponent and began making shots and marking his points on a small chalkboard hanging on the wall. He invited Danny to join them, but Danny didn't know how to play *bida*. He was pretty good at eight ball or straight pool, but these men were playing carom billiards. The tables did not even have pockets, and the game only used three balls. The scoring system depended on the cue ball banking off the cushions and hitting the other two balls. It seemed boring, yet Danny had seen players shout and argue and break cue sticks over each other like in any pool-room brawl.

After a while, Danny could not stand the smoke any longer. His lungs ached and his eyes burned. He walked outside and leaned against the brick wall, waiting for Sang Le to finish. Every nerve in his body prickled as he went over in his mind the words he would say to his cousin. The billiards, the smoking, the drinking were getting out of hand. Danny tried not to judge his cousin, and he knew he was having a tough time adjusting, but Sang Le would never graduate from high school if he kept on this course. His report card was proof of that.

Danny sighed and wished his cousin had not seen the *bida* room. The only video machine, an old Ms. Pac Man, was broken. There was nothing else to do, especially if you didn't smoke or drink. Every man inside had a pile of empty Budweiser cans on his table even though the store owner didn't have a license to sell beer. Old men sat at tables, smoking and arguing about the war. Young men smoked and argued about the billiards game.

As Danny watched the people coming and going from the Chinese movie house down the street, his back suddenly stiffened. The familiar small, trim figure of Cobra, followed by his three flunkies, emerged from around the corner and walked down the sidewalk in his direction. Danny quickly pushed off the brick wall and hurried inside.

"Sang Le, let's leave now," Danny whispered to his cousin, who had just marked his score on the small chalkboard nailed to the wall.

"No, no. I'm winning. Look, already I have some money." He raised his shirt. Danny gawked at the roll of one-dollar bills stuffed in Sang Le's waistband next to his skinny ribs.

"That's great, but somebody's coming down the street I don't want to talk to. Let's get out of here."

"I don't care who comes inside. The more players, the more chances I get to make money. I can put this in Bà's doggy bank." He patted the money through his shirt. "Maybe I don't need a job, if I can win like this all the time."

"You're just lucky today. You can't always win. You know that."

"It is not luck in *bida*. It is skill."

Danny spun around and saw Cobra walking through the door.

"Oh, brother," he moaned. "Sang Le, I swear, we have to get out of here. Please, come on."

But Sang Le shook his head stubbornly and continued his game. He drove his white cue ball across the felt at an angle. It bounced off an end cushion, then hit the red ball, then hit two side cushions, and finally tapped his opponent's white cue ball, all in rapid succession. A cheer rose from the small crowd that had gathered around Sang Le to admire his fantastic accuracy. He tallied his score on the chalkboard. He had won the whole game in only two turns.

"Well, well," Cobra's chubby friend said. "Did you bring some of your ugly sisters with you?" He ground a plump finger into Danny's chest.

"His sisters are not ugly," Sang Le said, grinning as he gathered his winnings. "They are very beautiful."

Cobra tilted his head back and laughed loudly, then shook hands with Sang Le.

"Hello, my brother," he said in Vietnamese, using the word that only the closest of friends used. His large smile looked out of place on his face.

Danny felt a wave of nausea roll through his stomach. He knew that Sang Le had met Cobra at least three times, including the day of the New Year's lion dance. But that was over a month ago. They must have met several other times, to be using such terms of friendship.

"You remember my little cousin, don't you, Tho?" Sang Le put a hand on Danny's back.

"Yes, I remember him very well." Cobra's small, black eyes bored into Danny. As before, Danny felt a chill creep up his spine. He couldn't imagine a name more appropriate for this man than Cobra.

"Sang Le, are you coming with me?" Danny asked.

Sang Le shook his head. "No. I want to stay and play *bida* with my friends."

"Let me buy you a beer, brother," Cobra said, as he put his hand on Sang Le's back.

Sang Le put his cue stick down, glancing over his shoulder at Danny. "Can my cousin join us?" he asked.

Cobra's lips turned up slightly. "Of course. Let me buy you a beer, too, Duong."

Danny shook his head. "I don't drink," he said abruptly and watched the black eyes grow darker. "Sang Le, what about the job you wanted? What should I tell Uncle Dao?"

"You need a job, brother?" Cobra's smooth, controlled voice purred from his throat. "Why didn't you tell me?"

"I was ashamed," Sang Le said.

"No problem, brother." Cobra paused to light a cigarette. His gold lighter twinkled in the pale light streaming from the swag lamp over the pool table. "I can get you a job like that." He snapped his fingers.

Danny felt a flash of anger. He couldn't stand it another minute. "Yeah, what kind of a job, Cobra?" he said. "Stealing social security checks from old women?"

Danny suddenly felt the weight of the fat boy pin him against the wall. He heard the click of a gun hammer.

"Want me to blow this smart-mouth away?"

"Now, now, my hotheaded friend, don't mistreat my brother's little cousin." Cobra laughed, jetting cigarette smoke from his nostrils.

Danny pushed the fat boy aside, then squared his shoulders. He clenched his fists to keep from punching the chubby face.

"Duong." Sang Le stepped closer. "Please, don't worry about me. And please don't wait. Take the bus home. I will come later. I am going to sit with my friend for a while and talk about Vietnam. There are plenty of shops and restaurants downtown. Surely Tho will find a job for me."

"That's what I'm afraid of," Danny muttered under his breath as he turned the collar up on his windbreaker and hurried out of the billiards hall. All the way to his uncle's video store, Danny wanted to kick himself for what had happened. He should have stood up to Cobra more. He should have told him to leave Sang Le alone. But instead he had acted like a scared rabbit.

Danny walked faster, his brain racing. Should he turn around and go back or just forget the whole thing? Should he tell his parents or Bà that Sang Le was becoming friends with a hoodlum, or just leave it alone? Danny didn't like to interfere with other people's business, and he hated them interfering with his. Didn't his cousin have the right to choose his own friends? How would he feel if Sang Le told Bà about Tiffany Marie?

He didn't know for a fact that Cobra was a lawbreaker. Cobra looked the part and everyone knew that gangs harassed shop owners downtown and fought over territory. His father had been in a sandwich shop the day a young man was gunned down at Vietnam Plaza in broad daylight. But no one was ever caught; it could have been a personal feud. So what if Cobra had the eyes of a devil? Having wicked looks was no crime.

By the time Danny reached Uncle Dao's video store, his steps were slow and even. He had decided he would not say anything to his parents or Bà for now. He would take Sang Le aside, explain that Cobra probably wasn't a very nice guy, and convince his cousin to get his grades back on course. He would be more patient with his cousin and try harder to help him find a job, even if it meant giving up the chance of finding a job for himself. He would *sacrifice* once again. After all, Sang Le had sacrificed for him. If for no other reason than that, Danny would not tell on his cousin.

The first thing Danny noticed as he stepped inside the video/record shop was that the usual

Vietnamese music was not playing—no Elvis Phuong or Vietnamese renditions of Madonna or the Everly Brothers, or a woman belting out a French love tragedy. He saw Vietnamese magazines and posters of Chinese actors strewn all over the floor.

Then he heard Aunt Lien crying hysterically. She sat behind the cashier's counter, pressing a dampened paper towel to her neck. Uncle Dao was leaning over her, holding a screaming baby in one arm and a whimpering toddler in the other.

"What happened?" Danny called out as he rushed across the store.

"*Toan du dang!* Look what they do to me!" Lien cried. She held up her delicate hands. Each long red fingernail had been cut off close to the quick.

"Why they do this to me?" she half cried, half screamed. As she lifted the red-stained paper towel, a thin line of blood trickled from a small knife incision on her ivory-smooth neck.

"But why?" Danny asked.

"They say we have to pay money or they will kill my babies and tear up our shop." Uncle Dao almost spat the words out.

Aunt Lien snatched the children up and ran. But even from the back of the store, Danny could still hear her muffled sobs.

"Who did this? What gang was it?" Danny asked. He tried to swallow the tremor in his voice.

"Ran-ho-mang." Uncle Dao hissed the words. He made a fist with two fingers protruding, then struck the air. Danny was unfamiliar with the Vietnamese words, but he didn't have to ask for a translation. There was no mistaking the strike of a cobra.

Chapter Nine

Sang Le did not come home that night or the next day, either. Danny found himself lying to Bà to protect his cousin. He told her that Sang Le was ashamed of his report card and felt too dishonored to face her. This only endeared Sang Le to the old woman more. She admired him for feeling shame and losing face. It proved he was not Americanized yet.

Danny confronted his cousin the next time he saw him—Monday morning as they rode on the bus. Calvin tried to persuade Sang Le, too, but Sang Le refused to believe that Cobra had anything to do with Uncle Dao's troubles. He moved to the back of the bus that day. At lunch he didn't join Danny and Calvin. He did not come to the cafeteria at all. And the avoidance continued for two weeks.

Although Sang Le had failed every subject except art and P.E., Bà chose not to be disappointed in her oldest grandson. She completely empathized with the difficulties he was going through. She had tried to learn English once herself and had given up in frustration, convinced that it was the most confusing language on earth, just as American society was the most confusing she had ever encountered.

Danny did not get off so lightly. In spite of the A on his science project, when his parents saw his history grade, they made him kneel in front of the family altar and reflect on his life for an hour every day. In all respects it looked like it was going to be a dark, gloomy month.

But suddenly everything in Danny's life changed: he turned sixteen, he passed his driver's test, and the very next day he found a job. A Chinese fish vendor only four blocks away needed someone to cut and clean fish. It was disgusting, smelly work, and Danny didn't tell any of his friends except Calvin what he did, but at least it was a real paying job. And he got to bring home fish every day, a fact that did not go unnoticed by Bà. Although she complained about the size and kind and quality of the fish, she did smile and grunt her approval once in a while.

On Friday, just before the final bell rang, Calvin and Danny stood in the hall near the physics lab.

"Man, that was a killer physics test," Calvin said and pretended to wipe beads of sweat from his forehead. "My brain cells feel all shriveled up."

"Well, at least we got out a little early today."

"Man, I'm parched. Go buy me a Coke. I'll save us a seat on the bus."

Danny shook his head. "Can't, Cal, I've gotta talk to my cousin."

"He still mad at you?"

"I think so. That's why I'm going to corner him in his art class. I want to hash this out and clear the air once and for all. Wanna come with me?"

"No thanks. I don't want to be there when you two start your kung fu fighting." He spun in the middle of the floor, faked a drop kick along with Bruce Lee-like squeals, then began singing the song "Kung Fu Fighting."

Danny sparred with Calvin a minute, then trotted to the art classroom. The smell of oils, acrylics, and turpentine penetrated the air, reminding him as it always did of finger paints in the first grade. Sang Le was busily putting finishing touches on a watercolor sketch. He was so absorbed he had not even heard the bell or noticed the other students cleaning brushes and pens and closing up.

The teacher, Mrs. Kendrick, smiled at Danny and waved him over.

"Come look at what your cousin is working on," she whispered. She tiptoed closer, as if the very sound of shoes would disturb Sang Le's concentration. "Isn't that the most beautiful watercolor you've ever seen?" she asked, her large hazel eyes peering at the pale colors. The scene was of two young Vietnamese girls in billowy long pants and traditional long, snug-fitting *ao dai* tunics. One girl carried a delicate umbrella over her shoulder; the other was leaning over the rail of the bridge they were standing on. Below them, on the river surface, hundreds of pink lotus blossoms floated. Farther away, standing men steered small boats with long bamboo poles.

"Sang Le is my most talented student," she said.

"Hey, that's beautiful, Sang Le," Danny said in awe. "Where is that?"

"Song Huong—the River of Perfumes in Hue."

"The old imperial city where Bà was born.

Is that the emperor's palace in the background?"

"Yes," Sang Le replied in Vietnamese. "We used to visit there as young children. Don't you remember? Once while you were trying to pick a lotus pod you slid into the moat. My back was turned when I heard a splash. I turned and saw your eyes, wide open, staring up at me from under the water's surface. You were perfectly still, as if in shock. I just reached in and grabbed your collar and lifted you out. You never cried or said a word. Then I foolishly slipped and fell in myself, and you laughed."

Danny felt heat creep to his face. It was the first time Sang Le had mentioned the familiar story. He wondered if his cousin would speak of what happened next. Would he complain that his mother's and father's and his own life had been ruined because of that moment of sacrifice to save the life of a small, careless boy?

"I don't exactly remember being there," Danny said, "but Bà has told me the story at least a hundred times. You were a real hero."

Sang Le shrugged. "I was a careless fool. It was my fault you fell in. My mother told me to watch you closely and not let you out of my sight. But I turned away to look at a little boat moving down the river, a *ghe* loaded with fruits from the mountains. A tribesman held a trained monkey on a rope. It sat in the middle of the boat eating bananas. If I had been doing my duty that day, perhaps my life would not be what it is. Perhaps my parents would still be alive. I often lay awake at night thinking about it. I have finally decided that bad spirits were punishing me for disobeying my mother."

Danny swallowed hard. Never in his wildest dreams had he thought that Sang Le would blame himself for the bad luck. A wave of affection swept over him.

"I'm sorry I was the cause of so much trouble." Danny forced a smile and placed his hand on his cousin's shoulder. "I guess I'll always be in your debt."

Though his eyes glistened, Sang Le grinned from ear to ear. He threw his skinny arms around Danny's shoulders and squeezed with all his might.

"Thank you, cousin."

"Well," Danny said as he shifted his weight uncomfortably and rubbed his nose, "we'd better hurry or we'll miss the bus. I've got to be at Cheng's Fish Market early today. Mr. Cheng says Friday is always a busy day for him."

Sang Le nodded and dabbed the last splash of watercolor on the paper.

"Cousin Duong, you work too much. You

always study so hard," he said. "This is Friday night. Everyone else in school is going on a date." He quickly washed his paintbrushes and put the supplies away. The American word "date" sounded odd in the middle of the Vietnamese sentence.

"Not me, cousin," Danny replied as they started down the almost empty corridor and stepped out the side door. "Not Calvin Pickney. How about you? Don't tell me you've got a date tonight?"

Sang Le grinned and nodded at the same time. "Tomorrow night. Big date," he said in broken English. "Double date."

"Oooh, double date. Twice the fun, huh." Danny poked his elbow into his cousin's ribs. "Don't tell me, let me guess who she is. Uh, Madonna? No, well, then it must be Hong Pham. Am I right?"

"She has finally honored me by saying yes. Her uncle has granted his permission for me to take her to dinner."

"And who's the other half of the double date? I guess it's her sister Cuc and some geeky computer guy."

"No, no. The other half of the date is you, cousin."

"What!" Danny screeched as they climbed

up into the bus. "You're crazy." Danny saw Calvin spread out in the back, his stuff on one seat, his long legs stretched out on another. On Fridays the bus was usually half-empty, because so many students had already left for jobs or skipped school.

"You have to come with us, Duong," Sang Le continued as he settled down in front of Cal. "I don't have a driver's license."

"Well, I've only had my license a few days, you know. And where would we get a car? Besides, I have to work all day and I'll smell like fish." Danny spewed out as many excuses as he could think of, but Sang Le had an answer for every one. He had already arranged to borrow a car from someone. Even Danny's mother had agreed to the date because she liked Hong very much and was glad that Sang Le was interested in such a sweet girl.

"You need date, Duong. You too mad and worry all time."

Danny sighed and fell back against the seat. "Look, I appreciate you worrying about my social life, but frankly, I don't think having a double date with Cuc would improve my disposition. It might even make me want to go out and shoot someone afterwards."

Sang Le shook his head. "No, no, date not

Cuc. I find very nice girl for you. Very pretty. Not Cuc. American call it blind date, but she not blind."

Calvin slapped his leg and roared with laughter. "Better listen to your cousin, man. He's got good taste. I saw him talking to a fine-looking girl today."

Danny moaned. It seemed that everyone in town knew about his blind date except for him. He heaved another sigh and closed his eyes tight while Sang Le continued to rattle off all the things he had planned for the date. A dinner at Kim Son Vietnamese restaurant, dancing at the Ritz nightclub afterwards.

Suddenly Danny was aware of a long silence. He opened one eye and saw that Sang Le was glaring at him, cross-armed.

"Cousin Duong, I don't like to do this, but remember I saved your life once. You owe me this favor."

Danny couldn't keep from smiling. He got up just as the bus slowed in front of the apartment complex. The elementary school kids had already gotten home and were running wild in the parking lot.

"Okay, cousin. If you put it that way, I guess I can't refuse. But don't expect me to be nice to Cuc. And don't tell me she won't be there. And don't *you* say another word." He pointed to Calvin who was bent over with laughter and slapping the seat.

When Danny got home Saturday afternoon, he took three baths, scrubbing his hands with deodorant soap until he thought his skin would peel off. But the stench of fish still clung to his hands. A splash of cologne helped; at least *his* nose couldn't smell it anymore.

Sang Le wasn't home. This didn't bother Danny too much, but as the time set for the date grew closer, he found himself pacing the floor. He knew it would be Cuc, and he was ready to accept that it would be a terrible date. He told himself he was doing it for Sang Le, for the time he had saved his life, for all the years his cousin had suffered in re-education camp and in the refugee camp in Hong Kong, for the humiliation he suffered in his school classes for not understanding English. His cousin deserved some happiness.

"Cousin, are you ready?"

Danny spun around. Sang Le was dressed in black pants, a white silk shirt, and an ugly striped tie. All the clothes belonged to Uncle Dao. Danny had seen them for the past five years at every wedding, funeral, or party his uncle attended.

"You look nice, Sang Le," Danny said.

"Hurry, cousin. My friend just dropped off his car for us to use."

Danny quickly kissed his mother good-bye and bounded down the concrete stairs to the parking lot. He glanced around, trying to spot the car a friend of Sang Le might own. He imagined it would be an older model, something like his father's car, but the only car in the lot he didn't recognize was a new, luxurious white BMW.

"Over here." Sang Le quickly pointed a remote control box at the BMW and pressed the button. It chirped as the alarm system disengaged.

"You've got to be kidding. This car?"

"Yes, we must be careful with it. My friend would be very unhappy if we wreck it."

As Danny slid onto the soft leather seat, he breathed in the aroma of pine air freshener and fresh new leather. Danny didn't see a single speck of dirt. He imagined that Sang Le had spent the past two hours washing, waxing, and cleaning the car.

Danny's enthusiasm grew with each minute he steered the car. He decided that maybe a date with Cuc would be worth the joy of driving an expensive car. Sang Le directed Danny to Hong's apartment complex, which was not very far away. A lot of Vietnamese families lived there.

Danny was not surprised at all when Sang Le returned to the car with Hong and Cuc on his arm. Danny drew in a deep breath, then let it out. He forced a smile at the sour-faced Cuc, who glared at him from under her thick eyebrows. She slid into the backseat next to her sister, obviously not wanting to be close to either of the boys. Thank goodness for small miracles, Danny whispered under his breath, quoting something that Calvin's mother often said.

"You look very nice," Sang Le said to Hong in perfect English. "That color good for you."

"Thank you," she said in a demure voice. Danny glanced over his shoulder and saw her dark eyes looking at him. His cousin was right. Hong did look great in a Mandarin-collared pink silk dress covered with delicate white flowers. It fit the contours of her body snugly, and Danny was surprised to see that she had a nice figure and wasn't as flat-chested as he had remembered. Her hair looked different, too, and sported an artificial white flower that complemented her smooth complexion. Cuc, on the other hand, wore the same dress she had been wearing at the supermarket the first time he met her. Her hair was pulled back slick from her face with a red ribbon, making her cheeks and chin look even more starkly chiseled.

"Okay, where to next, cousin? Kim Son Restaurant?"

"No, we have to go someplace else first. Take a right on this next street."

Danny followed his cousin's instructions, wondering what was happening. They were traveling in the opposite direction of Beechnut Street, where the restaurant was located. When his cousin directed him to turn left, recognition flashed through Danny's mind.

"Where are we going, cousin?" he asked. "This is not the way to any restaurant I know about. This is a residential neighborhood." Danny's gaze swept over the rows of small, neat brick houses built in the 1950s. The kind that wouldn't have automatic dishwashers or central air-conditioning, unless they had been remodeled. They all looked the same except for the color of the brick and wood trim and the style of the front porches. He knew at least three students who lived on this street, including Tiffany Marie Schultz. And he knew there were no restaurants or anything slightly resembling entertainment for several blocks.

"Are you sure this is the right street?"

"Very sure, cousin Duong," Sang Le replied.

He leaned over the driver's seat and pointed a long finger toward a tan-colored brick house with fresh-looking brown trim. Danny swallowed hard.

"What's going on?" Danny felt his heart skip as Sang Le told him to stop in front of the driveway. "What are we doing here?" Danny's voice was quivering. He coughed lightly.

"This is your blind date. She not really blind." Sang Le laughed. "Go ahead and knock on door. Please."

Danny let the air from his lungs. This couldn't be happening. What had his cousin done? How could Sang Le have possibly arranged a blind date with Tiffany Schultz? He hardly knew her and certainly didn't speak English well enough to communicate with her. Danny shook his head and groaned under his breath. After tonight she would probably never speak to him again.

"I can't go in there. Are you crazy? Does she know it's me the blind date is with?"

"Sure. I told her we go to nice Vietnamese restaurant. She say she never eat Vietnamese food. She want to go very bad. Go ahead, knock on door. I wait here."

Danny glanced at his pants and shirt. He had not even bothered to dress in his best clothes. He had been so sure that his blind date would be Cuc. He took a quick look at the backseat where Cuc sat stiffly next to the door. Suddenly he realized that she was Hong's chaperon. In Vietnam, decent girls did not go out alone with boys. Always an older relative or friend accompanied them.

"This is going to be some date," Danny muttered as he walked up the neatly trimmed sidewalk lined with clumps of yellow and purple pansies and one huge azalea bush smothered with bright pink blooms. The house was dark except for the kitchen and what must have been the living room. As he paused at the door, Danny heard laughter coming from a TV program. He rang the bell and heard a dog bark in the backyard.

There was the sound of voices and clatter inside before the door opened. Danny sucked in air. Tiffany was knock-dead beautiful. She looked perfect in her tight faded jeans, a fuzzy soft blue sweater, and big dangling earrings.

"Hi, Danny," she said, inviting him in.

Danny stepped inside the room. It wasn't exactly what he had expected. The furniture was pretty old. A flowered sheet had been tossed over the sofa and the carpet was stained and almost threadbare near the entrance. Books and odds and ends filled nearly every corner, making it look junky. But the thing that amazed him the most was who he saw sitting in front of the television—a boy in a wheelchair. He looked to be about twelve, but with his withered legs it was hard to tell. The boy laughed occasionally at a sitcom.

The deep-throated barking continued from the backyard until someone shouted from the kitchen. A moment later a middle-aged, blond-haired woman came in, wiping her hands on a paper towel. Her face was still attractive, though she had lost her figure. Her stout thighs seemed to stretch her white nurse's uniform to the limit. Her shoes lay in the middle of the floor and her feet were covered with white support hose. Danny was surprised to see her strike a match and light up a cigarette. You would think a nurse wouldn't smoke.

"Hi, I'm Tiffany's mother," she said, holding out her hand. She saw Danny staring at the cigarette and shrugged. "I'm going to quit tomorrow," she said with a husky laugh. "So what are you guys going to do tonight?"

"Uh, we're going to a Vietnamese restaurant, then skating," Tiffany said. "Uh, excuse me a minute while I get my purse."

Danny noticed that the boy had turned in

his seat at the mention of skating. His eyes, large and blue like Tiffany's, stared at Danny. But as soon as the commercial was over, he turned back to the program.

"I'm so glad Tiffany is going out," her mother said as she watched her daughter disappear into a bedroom. "She needs a break." The woman glanced at the wheelchair, then took Danny's arm and steered him to the hallway out of the boy's hearing range.

"Tiffany doesn't get to date very much. She has to watch after Bradley. I just can't afford to hire a sitter. I work nights so I can be with him during the days. Tiffany watches him at night. For once she asked me to switch shifts with another nurse so she could go on this date. I said, this Danny must really be something special. I can see why she likes you."

Danny stared at the floor and felt his face blush. When he looked up, he saw Tiffany standing in the hall, her own face red. She quickly smiled and hurried over to Danny.

"Well, I hope you weren't talking about me," she kidded. "Mom, we won't be out too late." She kissed her mother, leaving a pale pink image on the woman's left cheek. "Don't forget, Bradley needs his medicine at exactly eight o'clock. Don't let him talk you out of it. And no caffeine in his Cokes. He'll try to tell you it won't keep him up, but it will."

"Yes, Herr Doktor," the woman said in a phony German accent and gave a snappy military salute. "Don't worry about Bradley. I think I can handle the little monster one night. You two have fun." As she opened the door, her eyes grew round. "My, that's a beautiful car, Danny. Does it belong to your folks?"

"Uh, no, it belongs to a friend of the family."

"Well, have fun." She waved and closed the door.

Tiffany smiled again. "You know how mothers are. They have to know everything they can about the guys their daughters are dating."

"Your mom is nice. I'm surprised she didn't tell you to be in by midnight or something like that."

"Oh, she knows I won't stay out late. I'm not the irresponsible type."

Danny opened the door for her and then ran around to the driver's seat. For the first time, the fact that he was really going out on a date with Tiffany hit him. His heart pounded and his fingers shook. Suddenly he couldn't remember how to drive. He put the car into the wrong gear, and the car shot backward, barely missing a pickup parked along the curb. Everyone laughed except for Hong, who whispered something to her sister, then grew very quiet.

Danny drove to Kim Son Restaurant, where they settled around a table with an electric hot plate in its center. Although his cousin, Hong, and Cuc spoke only Vietnamese, Tiffany didn't seem to mind. Sang Le ordered and soon one waiter brought out a huge pot of spicy-flavored boiling water and placed it on the hot plate, while another waiter brought a tray covered with strips of raw pork, beef, shrimp, fishballs, squid, vegetables, and thin bean filament noodles. Danny and Sang Le dropped pieces of meat into the pot and removed them a few minutes later when they were lightly cooked, constantly adjusting the heat of the hot plate. Tiffany tried everything, no matter how strange it looked or tasted to her. She didn't like the squid, but she didn't make faces like Calvin always did. And she broke into giggles every time she tried to handle the chopsticks. Danny had to teach her how. The touch of her soft, warm hand felt heavenly.

Sang Le was bubbling over, too. He served Hong as if she were a princess, putting her meat into the boiling water and withdrawing it expertly with chopsticks and placing it in a small bowl. It would be bad luck to put it directly on her plate. Cuc, who sat on the other side of her sister, had to serve herself.

Afterwards in the car, Sang Le said in his clearest English. "Now we go to Ritz Club."

"The Ritz Club. What is that?" Tiffany asked.

"A Vietnamese dance club."

"Oh, but I'm not dressed for dancing. I thought Sang Le said we were going skating."

"No, no. I say dancing," Sang Le said.

"Oh, I'm sorry, I thought you said skating." Danny saw the cloud of confusion on Tiffany's face and wanted to scream. She probably had not understood his heavy accent. It was a small miracle he had communicated the concept of a blind date to her.

"It's okay, we'll go skating first," Danny said as he started the motor. "We'll go dancing afterwards. The Ritz doesn't even open until ten P.M. anyway."

Danny heard Cuc grunt and whisper to Hong in Vietnamese. "If I knew we were going skating, I would not have worn a dress. I would not have come at all. I would much rather go dancing." Danny thought that no guy would ask her to dance anyway.

The Starlite Skating Rink was packed. Most of the teenagers inside were Vietnamese. While rock-and-roll music blasted their ears, Tiffany and Danny tried to skate. The crowd made it difficult, but she was very good and they managed to stay by each other's sides. During the couples-only skating, they held hands. Danny had never felt happier in his life.

Sang Le knew nothing about skating, but this didn't stop him from trying. He fell again and again, but soon had learned enough to go around without too much trouble. But in spite of efforts to persuade Hong and Cuc to get on the floor, the two sisters refused to budge from the side bench. The most adventuresome thing they did all night was to go to the snack bar and buy ice cream bars.

Danny noticed that Hong's dark eyes followed him and Tiffany every time they rounded the curve nearest the snack bar. She stared at Tiffany with a burning intensity that bordered on rudeness. During couples skating, while the lights were off and the big twirling ball sent shimmering colored light onto the floor, Danny stole a quick kiss. When he looked up he saw Hong's face. Maybe it was just the lights, but he thought she looked as pale as a ghost.

Danny had expected Cuc to have a frown on her face, but when they all piled into the car, Hong seemed just as annoyed and grumpy as her sister.

"We are ready to go home now," she said in Vietnamese. There was no denying the quiver in her voice.

Sang Le's smile suddenly dropped.

"I thought we were going dancing at the Ritz," he said softly. "We were going to dance the cha-cha, remember?" Sang Le's eyes glistened with warmth, as they always did when he spoke to Hong.

"I don't feel like dancing," Hong said curtly. It was the only time Danny had heard such sharpness in her voice. He looked at Tiffany.

"Do you want to go dancing?" he asked.

"What kind of dancing?"

"Well, it's mostly the old-fashioned ballroom stuff—cha-cha, rumba, tango, fox-trot. But they play some fifties and sixties rock-and-roll, too—mostly jitterbug. You can dance cha-cha to the new wave disco they play. I could teach you the cha-cha basics in five minutes."

"I'm not really dressed for dancing. But I could sit with you and watch them dance." She reached over and squeezed Danny's hand.

"No!" There was no mistaking the aggravation in Hong's voice this time. "I have to go home now." She turned to her sister and spoke angrily in Vietnamese. Danny only caught a few phrases like "that American girl" and "dancing with him." A flash of anger exploded inside his heart. He wished he had never rescued the sisters from Cobra at the market that day.

"Cousin Duong," Sang Le said in Vietnamese, "I think we should take Hong and Cuc home now. They can't go dancing after all. Sorry."

"That's okay, I understand." He turned to Tiffany. "Uh, there's been a complication. The girls have to get home, so we can't go dancing tonight. Maybe next weekend. You can pick an American dance club."

Tiffany nodded. If she was disappointed, she hid it well. But in spite of the sisters' joint foul moods—each now sat in icy silence with folded arms in the backseat—Danny considered the date a success. He had held Tiffany's hand most of the time during skating, stolen one little kiss, and now she snuggled close to him and looped her arm through his.

They were closest to Tiffany's house, so they dropped her off first. Danny didn't want to, but since it wasn't his car he couldn't protest too loudly.

Danny pulled to the curb. This time the 1967 red Mustang convertible—the one in his favorite photograph—was in the driveway.

"My brother Frank is home," Tiffany said. Danny felt her back stiffen. She slid her arm from his and scooted to the far side of the passenger seat.

"I'll walk you to the door," Danny said.

"No, no, that's all right. You don't have to."

Danny's eyebrows crinkled. "Well, I can't just drop you off like a hitchhiker," he said as he opened his door and hurried to the other side of the car. Tiffany had already opened her door and was on the sidewalk. He had to trot to catch up with her.

"Tiffany, is something wrong?" he asked as he took her arm. "Did I say something to make you mad? Is it the dancing? I'm sorry about that. Those girls are crazy. They decided they can't dance. The next time we go out, I promise we'll be alone. I mean, there will be a next time, won't there?"

Tiffany spun and faced him. "I really like you, Danny. It wasn't anything you said or did. And I don't care about the dancing."

"Then what is it?"

"My brother. He gets kind of crazy sometimes. He never approves of any of the guys I date."

"Is he your boss?"

"Well . . . yes, I guess he is. We don't have a father."

"Oh, sorry. I didn't know your father was dead."

She stared at the ground for a few seconds, then slowly exhaled.

"He's not dead. He left us about four years after Bradley was born. Mom says he just couldn't take the responsibility of a disabled child. Since then, Frank has been the man of the house."

"Well, surely he lets you date once in a while."

"Frank's gotten mixed up with some pretty weird guys lately. He comes and goes as he pleases. To tell you the truth, Mom can't control him anymore. He's too big and too strong. He's not a bad person, really. He used to be nice, but that creep he hangs out with, Brian . . . oh well."

"Frank can't keep you from dating forever. Hey, the prospects won't get any better than me." Danny stretched his arms out and turned around. It had the effect he had hoped for. Tiffany laughed and punched him lightly on the shoulder.

"Oh, okay, you can walk me to the door. Maybe he's asleep."

"I don't think so. Nobody could sleep through that kind of music." As they strolled closer to the house, heavy metal music pulsated out of an open side window. It wasn't too loud, but an electric guitar screamed out high-pitched, annoying notes. The light was on and the curtains were pulled back. Danny saw posters on the walls, mostly of heavy metal bands, and one of a man in a German helmet with a swastika above it.

As they stepped onto the porch the dog barked again. Danny heard a boy shouting at the dog to shut up, then the sounds of two other boys laughing and heckling.

"You'd better go. I mean it, Danny. Frank has some of his weird friends in there with him. They are *really* creepy." She hesitated a second, then smiled. "I had a wonderful time." She leaned forward and kissed him on the cheek, then turned. On an impulse, Danny pulled her back and kissed her lips. He caught her off guard and half missed, but she returned the embrace for a few seconds.

"Anh yeu em," he whispered.

"What does that mean?" she asked.

"It means . . ." Danny paused. He wished he had the nerve to tell her what it really meant, *I love you,* but he couldn't yet. "It means you're beautiful, Tiffany," he lied.

"Thank you, Danny. So are you." She looked into his eyes, then opened the door and vanished inside.

Danny ran all the way to the car, his heart doing flip-flops. As he started the motor, he saw three teenage boys and one who was in his twenties come to the open front door and stare. He saw their shaved heads and the tattoos on their arms and the heavy military boots. Calvin had been right. They did look like skinheads. They shouted something about "chinks" and walked toward the car, but Danny gunned the gas pedal. The car sped away.

Danny was in a dream world as he drove the girls home, even though everyone else in the car was in a gloomy mood. Nothing Sang Le said would make Hong speak. And Cuc only complained.

After dropping the sisters off, Sang Le moved into the front seat next to Danny.

"What happened to Hong?" Danny asked. "She was all happy when we first picked her up. She got mad about something at the skating rink, didn't she?"

"You are blind, little cousin. Can't you see what was wrong with her?"

"Was it because she couldn't skate and felt left out? I was worried about that."

"That was just a small part of it."

"Was it because she was wearing a dress and felt out of place?"

"No, that wasn't the main reason."

"Then was it because she couldn't dance? Is that why she didn't want to go to the Ritz?"

"No. She practiced her cha-cha every night this week just for this occasion."

"I get it. She was mad because she *didn't* get to go dancing."

"No. She truly did change her mind and did not want to go."

"Then what? I'm out of guesses."

"It's you, little cousin."

"What?"

"It is you, Duong, that she likes. She wanted to be the one to skate with you and she wanted to be the one to dance with you. I did not tell her that we were going to pick up Tiffany for your date. She only came on this date because she hoped that you would learn to like her as much as she likes you."

"Oh, man. I don't believe that. I told you she's not my type. Is she blind? Can't she see that you're head over heels in love with her? You waited on her hand and foot tonight."

"Yes," Sang Le said, expelling a long ragged sigh. "I feel that way about her, but she does not care for me. She is perfect in every way. She is beautiful, quiet, sweet, and talented. She would make a perfect wife. I love her deeply, Duong. But it is *you* she loves."

"Man, I don't know what to say. You know I don't like Hong. I like Tiffany. Why don't you just tell Hong that?"

"I think she knows it now. And she will probably never speak to me again. She had only been my friend because I am your cousin. Who would want a skinny, ugly guy like me with no money and no future? I cannot even get a high school diploma or a job. I should have stayed in Vietnam." He slammed his fist on the dashboard.

"Don't say that, Sang Le. We'll work this out somehow. You'll find a job as soon as you get your driver's license."

"I can't pass the test if I can't read English."

"We'll try one more time," Danny said as he steered the white car into the apartment parking lot. "You're too hard on yourself, Sang Le. Just give it a little time." He turned the ignition off and handed the keys to his cousin. "Thanks for a great blind date. It was terrific. I owe you another favor."

"Well, I am pleased that you are happy. At least someone enjoyed this night." As Danny got out of the car, Sang Le slid over into the driver's seat and started up the ignition. "I am returning the car to my friend. I will see you later tonight."

Danny watched the car disappear down the road. Even though his cousin didn't have his license, he was a very good driver.

Danny tossed and turned until two o'clock, thinking of Tiffany Marie. Everything had felt so natural and right with her. He had thought he would be at a loss for words on a date with Tiffany, but she was easy to talk to. They had a lot more in common than he had realized and she was really interesting. She made him feel like a king. He'd dated other girls, even thought he was in love with Leticia Quiroz, a cute Filipina, until she became a cheerleader and dumped him. But nothing had ever come close to the feeling he had when he was with Tiffany. Danny thought about the feel of her soft, fuzzy sweater on his fingers and the warm smell of her perfume. A tiny hint of the fragrance still lingered on his shirt where she had rested her head. He put the shirt close to his face and breathed deeply. Soon he was asleep, dreaming about fields of wildflowers and Tiffany Marie in his arms.

At five A.M. Danny awoke to a noise. He saw his cousin slipping through the bedroom door and smelled the stench of beer. Danny flipped on the lamp.

"Hey, Sang Le, where have you been?" he asked in a gravelly voice. "Bà was asking about you."

"What did you tell her?" Sang Le asked, his glazed-over eyes squinting at the light.

"I told her you were spending the night with

a friend. She must have thought I meant Hong. She's pretty upset. You'd better talk to her in the morning."

"Don't worry, cousin Duong. I have a good explanation. I've got a job. A very good job. Look." He pulled a wad of money from his pants pocket and dumped the crumpled bills onto his bed. He lost his balance, then plopped on top of the money and giggled.

"What kind of job?" Danny asked, sitting up and staring at the crumpled bills. He saw at least two twenties.

"A night job. They pay extra for working at night."

"What's the name of the company?"

"Ah, I don't exactly know. It's Chinese. They make bags for holding rice. A friend got the job for me. I will show you someday. I work with equipment repair, like your father. Please, I am very tired. I will sleep now."

Danny flipped the lamp off. He stared at the shadows of trees dancing on the ceiling wall and could not sleep. He wanted to believe his cousin, but how could he? What kind of job paid you in wadded-up cash the first night? And what kind of job would let its employees drink beer? Maybe Sang Le had cashed his first check and then celebrated his new job with a friend.

Danny rolled over. Maybe he was naive to think that was the answer, but he didn't want to think who the "friend" really was and what the job might be. If Danny thought about it too much, he knew that any other explanation would mean something far worse.

Chapter Ten

Easter came late that year. March had blown out wild and blustery, giving way to a rainy April. Already the temperatures had risen to the eighties and Danny dug out his summer shorts and tank tops. Every chance he got, he lifted weights at Calvin's house. He wanted to look good for Tiffany.

Danny yawned and stretched in his bed the Friday before Easter, basking in the luxury of sleeping late for the holiday. He smiled as he thought about Tiffany. A lot of things had happened since their blind date almost a month ago. They spent as much time together as possible, even though they had not had another "official" date. Tiffany moved to the back of the history class next to Danny; she sat next to him during lunch, even though it meant putting up with Calvin's constant jibes. Danny phoned her every night. A couple of Sundays when Tiffany's mother didn't have to work, they met at the library and worked on research papers. One day their history class toured the museum downtown to look at a Native American exhibit, and Danny stole a kiss behind the headdress of Satanta, chief of the Kiowas.

The closest they came to having real dates was during spring break in March. Every day for a week, Danny took Tiffany and Bradley to a city park with two dilapidated tennis courts.

Danny sighed as he recalled Tiffany's strong, tanned legs dashing across the court. Most of the girls and women wore shorts, or even jeans, but Tiffany wore one of those little white outfits with a tiny pleated skirt. He loved the sexy way it flipped every time she smacked a forehand or sent a serve whistling through the air. Though petite, she had exceptional power and control. If she just had more time, Danny knew she could be on the tennis team. The thought of training with her or being her partner in mixed doubles made his heart race. Of course, that would never come true. She could not be on the team any more than he could, because of family obligations.

Danny got to know Bradley better, too, and genuinely liked the spunky kid. Brad played tennis with them, hitting balls right and left, able to steer his wheelchair with amazing dexterity. They had big plans for the Easter holiday. Danny was going to take Brad and Tiffany for a long drive in the country to look at bluebonnets and other wildflowers. They would drive to a small town about an hour and a half away and there meet Tiffany's grandparents at a restaurant. After eating, Danny would drive back to Houston alone, while Tiffany and Brad would ride on to their grandparents' farm three hours away. It was a ritual Tiffany and Brad honored every Easter. Usually Mrs. Schultz drove them. But this year she had to work the day shift and Frank didn't want to do anything as wimpy as look at wildflowers.

Danny had never seen the Texas countryside in spring, but Tiffany told him it was something else—palettes of blue, orange, yellow, and pink wildflowers carpeting empty pastures and roadsides. Danny wasn't much of a nature buff, but he'd do anything to spend an afternoon with Tiffany. At last his dream of strolling by her side through a fresh meadow was going to come true.

Danny rolled over and slowly got up. As usual, Sang Le's bed had not been slept in. It had been that way since the night of the double date. Sang Le had become a ghost in the household, slipping in early in the morning to catch one or two hours of sleep, then riding the bus to school. From there he would vanish into thin air. Danny had searched for him one day, only to find out from the ESL teacher that Sang Le had not been to class for two weeks.

Mrs. Kendrick, the art teacher, often cornered Danny in the hallway, asking about her truant student. Sang Le had left in the middle of an ambitious art project. She wanted to enter it in the annual citywide student art competition to be held in late May. Now she feared that he would not be able to finish it on time. She had even called the apartment a couple of times, only to get Bà or Danny's mother on the phone. She had eventually given up.

Danny couldn't deny that Sang Le was artistically talented—the bedroom wall was covered with his sketches and watercolors, mostly of Hong. Through Sang Le's eyes, Hong's ordinary beauty had been transformed into something magnificent and eternal. Mrs. Kendrick was a nice person, but Danny began to avoid her. He didn't know where his cousin was and resented people thinking he was lying about it.

A thump at his door and the sound of arguing brought Danny out of his daydreams. He rubbed his eyes and yawned again, then dressed for work. He opened the door and saw Bà and Kim fighting again. This time Kim wanted to go to Memorial Park with some friends for a giant Easter egg hunt sponsored by a radio station. Bà wanted Kim to stay home and help prepare for the *thoi noi,* the "leaving the cradle" celebration, for Uncle Dao and Aunt Lien's little girl. One month after her birth the family had celebrated the baby's *dau thang*—a giving of thanks to the spirits for not taking back their precious gift before she was thirty days old. Now, at age one she would have the only birthday party of her life, at least until she reached sixty and had another party to celebrate reaching the age of wisdom.

Bà tried to get Danny to settle the argument, but he held up his hands and darted for the front door. "Sorry, no time to settle arguments today. I'm late for work."

Danny switched into a faster gait. He was lucky Cheng's Fish Market was only four blocks away. He could jog there and back every day and it helped to keep him in shape.

Work went well for Danny. He had learned quickly how to scale and gut the fish and had been promoted to fill in for the counter clerk during his days off. The fish market didn't use computerized cash registers. The cashiers had to know math well enough to make correct change. Danny excelled in math, so it was easy. Mr. Cheng was a good and fair boss. He told Danny that he would be getting a ten cents per hour raise starting with his next paycheck. It wasn't much, but at least Danny knew he had potential. If he worked full time during the summer, he could save up enough for his own car.

After work that evening, as Danny walked into the apartment parking lot, he recognized Uncle Dao's car and the cars of several family friends. The lights of the apartment glowed golden warm, and Danny heard laughter as he climbed the steps. He peeked through the picture window and saw the table lined with twelve bowls of green bean tapioca pudding and twelve plates of molded steamed sweet rice, symbolizing the twelve spirits of childbirth.

Bà had already announced the baby to the guests by her official name and wished her long life and happiness and prosperity. Now, in front of the baby girl sitting on the floor, Bà placed a tray of items—a rose, a comb, a pair of scissors, a pen, a ruler, a coin, rice, and a clod of dirt. Whatever the girl chose would determine her future. The child hesitated, then grabbed the rose. Everyone laughed and clapped—it meant she would be a big flirt.

Danny wanted to get cleaned up and retire early so he would be refreshed for the trip with Tiffany and Bradley tomorrow. As he walked to his bedroom, he saw Bà's dog bank laying on its side in the hall. He picked it up and noticed how light it felt.

Danny had never challenged his cousin about the night job. Maybe he was afraid of the answer. He was sure no one got paid nightly, and often the stench of beer lingered on Sang Le's breath. One night Danny had seen Sang Le stuffing a thick wad of money into the dog bank.

Danny started to put the dog in the hall closet, but on a sudden impulse, he carried it to his room and closed the door. It was one of those banks that had to be busted open to get the money out because it had no opening on the bottom. Danny picked up one of Sang Le's art brushes and slipped it into the slot and stirred the money around, then held it up to the light. He saw several twenties, tens, a few fives. He jiggled it some more, then saw a clump of hundreds. His stomach felt sick.

"Sang Le, what have you gotten yourself into," he said out loud.

The door softly clicked and Sang Le stepped inside.

"I have gotten myself into nothing, Duong," Sang Le said. He took the dog from Danny's hand, then crammed more bills through the slot.

"Where are you getting the money?" Danny asked. "I know you're not working at the rice bag factory. They barely pay minimum wage there."

Sang Le shrugged, then sat on the edge of the bed and removed his shoes and socks.

"I win the money playing *bida*. My talents are renowned. Every night someone challenges me. I rarely lose." He unbuttoned his shirt and stood. "Now please forgive me. I need to change clothes. I have some important things to do tonight."

Danny didn't believe his cousin. The men who came into the *bida* halls were not wealthy. They were just ordinary guys with ordinary jobs, who played to take their minds off their dreary lives. They arrived in old Chevys or banged-up Toyotas, not new BMWs.

Something was wrong with Sang Le's story. But for the moment Danny decided to accept it. Tonight he didn't want his cousin in the room;

he wanted to stretch out on his bed and call Tiffany and talk about their plans.

After his cousin left, Danny pulled the telephone cord as far as it would reach, settled down, and dialed Tiffany's number. A male answered, startling Danny. Her brother Frank was hardly ever home on Friday nights. Danny tried to shrug off his qualms and asked for Tiffany.

"Who is this?" the voice demanded.

"Danny."

There was the sound of the receiver scraping on a hard surface, then the boy shouting Tiffany's name.

"Hello," she said in a tiny, shaky voice.

"Hi, it's me."

"Danny? I told you to always hang up if my brother answers," she whispered. "He may be listening on the other line."

Anger exploded through Danny's heart. The only subject that he and Tiffany did not agree on, the only thing they ever fought about, was her brother Frank. It infuriated and frustrated Danny that she acted so scared of her older brother. For instance, earlier in the week as they each waited for their bus after school, her brother's red Mustang suddenly pulled up and revved its motor. Tiffany got a worried look in her eyes and dashed away. Of course, Danny ordered his own sisters around sometimes, and if they disobeyed he would chastise them—make them do extra chores, or ground them, or make them kneel in front of the altar. But never would he dream of physically hurting one of them, despite Kim's stubborn streak.

"We're not doing anything wrong," Danny protested. "We're just talking on the phone. Why do you always have to act so secretive around your brother? What's he going to do, beat you up if you date someone?" After he'd said the words, Danny felt awful. He had been in such a great mood; he hadn't meant to argue with Tiffany tonight. All he wanted to do was talk. Now he knew he'd hurt her feelings. It seemed that the closer they grew to each other, the more they argued about her brother.

"I'm sorry, Tiffany," Danny said with a sigh.

"Danny, you don't know everything that goes on in my house. You just don't know my brother."

"I know he's in some kind of skinhead gang."

"No! He's not in a gang. He just hangs out with a few guys that try to act tough. That Brian is a jerk, but Frank's really a sweet guy."

"All right, so he's not in a gang. But what does that have to do with you and me? You know, sometimes I think the main reason we haven't been out on another date is because you're afraid of what Frank might say."

"You know I have to watch Bradley."

"Yeah, and I also know that your mom does get a night off now and then. So, what is it, really?"

The silence grew painful, then Danny heard Tiffany draw in a deep breath.

"It's not just any date with any boy that Frank's opposed to—it's you, Danny. He hates Vietnamese people. Remember how I told you once that our father was in Vietnam?"

"Yes." Danny didn't like where this conversation was going. It wouldn't be the first time an American had blamed Danny for what happened to some loved one in the war twenty years ago. Suddenly he wished he'd never pressed her for an answer.

"Well, my dad got all messed up in the head. He was treated in the VA hospital for post-traumatic stress. That was before I was even born. He was okay for a long time, then after Bradley was born he kind of went crazy again. Mom says he never would have left us if he'd been right in the head. Anyway, Frank blames all Vietnamese for our dad leaving. I know it's crazy, but there it is. I'm sorry, Danny. I should have told you before now."

Danny expelled the air from his lungs slowly.

He imagined the big-boned, clumsy-looking Frank Schultz, with his short-cropped hair and sloppy clothes. Nobody in school liked him except for his gang buddies. All of them looked and acted alike—losers with bad tempers. Then he thought of Tiffany and her trim, petite figure. She and her mother would be hard-pressed to prevent Frank from hurting them if he had a mind to.

"Tiffany, we can't keep hiding the truth from Frank forever. He's going to find out sooner or later that we're seeing each other. I want us to spend a lot more time together, just you and me. And I don't mean at the library. You told me you feel the same way."

"I do, Danny, you know I do."

"Then ask your mom to take the day shift next Saturday and let's go out on a real date. A movie and dinner. Maybe we'll try the cha-cha at the Ritz."

"But we're going to see each other tomorrow."

"That's not a date. Brad and your grandparents will be there. Someone else is always with us when we go out. I want to be with you *alone* for once."

Danny heard a commotion on the other end of the line.

"I've got to go," Tiffany whispered. "Frank

just came back in. Talk to you later. Bye." The line clicked.

Danny slammed the receiver down. He had never felt so frustrated in his life. He knew Tiffany loved him as much as he loved her. After years of exchanging secretive glances and brief bits of conversation at school, finally they had both expressed their true feelings. He couldn't lose her now.

He thought about going to her house and confronting Frank Schultz. The guy was big and clumsy-looking, but he was intelligent. Frank's science fair project had come close to winning two years ago. Danny hadn't even known he was Tiffany's brother back then. Frank hadn't dressed or acted so weird, either. If Tiffany was smart, kind, and fair, surely Frank had inherited some of those family traits, too.

Danny rolled over and closed his eyes. He fell asleep dreaming of Tiffany Marie and the field of wildflowers. Just as he started to kiss her warm lips, Frank Schultz appeared and started chasing him with a knife dripping blood, screaming his name.

"Danny! Danny!"

Danny returned to consciousness with a painful jerk. He sat up to find bright lights blinding his eyes and excited voices calling his name.

Danny glanced at the clock on his desk. It was three A.M. He sat up and squinted at the worried faces hovering above him. "What's wrong?" he grumbled.

"Kim has run away."

Chapter Eleven

It was the longest nine days Danny had ever experienced, but at last the ordeal was over. Now, as he glanced over his shoulder at Kim safely asleep in the back seat of the car, curled up like a baby, he didn't know whether to kiss or kill his little sister. During that time, she had stayed in a run-down unfurnished apartment with an eighteen-year-old boy she hardly knew. As it turned out, he was the younger brother of one of Cobra's gang, and she had met him outside Queen Bee the night of Sang Le's arrival. It was Sang Le who had discovered where Kim was.

Danny was relieved that Kim had agreed to

come back home, but he found it hard to forgive this selfish child who had turned their whole household, and his life in particular, topsy-turvy. Danny had canceled his Easter plans with Tiffany, but he was too embarrassed to tell her why, except that it was a family emergency. He knew Tiffany didn't believe him, and he didn't blame her for being mad. If she had called him at home, he had not been there, and he didn't receive any messages.

He didn't see her at school, because he skipped every day to search for Kim. He missed a major history exam and quit his job to devote his time to the search. He carried guilt upon his shoulders like a heavy boulder, for he knew that Bà blamed him for Kim's behavior. In her eyes he had not been strict enough with the rebellious girl.

The family welcomed Kim back home with open arms. Everyone wept and laughed and talked over each other as they hugged her. Even the hard-hearted Kim shed a few tears when her father wrapped his arms around her. Danny's mother and Bà bustled in the kitchen preparing Kim's favorite foods and his father gave her a new stuffed animal for her immense collection.

There were too many people at the dining table, so Danny and Sang Le sat on the sofa in front of the television. The ten o'clock news came on with a reporter announcing another murder in Chinatown. She spoke into a microphone as the camera zoomed in on ambulance attendants loading a body onto a stretcher.

"Tsh!" Danny's mother said and waved a hand toward the TV as she walked across the room to get another chair for the table. "Those bad *toan du dang* are killing each other off. Good. I hope they all die." She spat the words out and turned her back on the TV screen.

The camera swept across the crowd gathered on the sidewalk. Danny recognized Cobra's chubby friend, then he saw Nguyen Thơ himself, looking pale and skinny in the background. Danny squinted and strained at another person in the crowd wearing a Cobra jacket. Danny swallowed hard then quickly glanced at his parents to see if they had recognized Sang Le's face also. Everyone was looking away from the TV except for Bà and he knew her eyes were too old to see clearly.

Danny felt sick and suddenly lost his appetite. He laid his plate on the coffee table and looked at his cousin. Sang Le pushed his plate aside, too, then lit up a cigarette and stared straight ahead.

Danny shifted his weight, then drew in a deep breath.

"Sang Le . . . cousin . . . do you know how much it would break our grandmother's heart if she learned that you were a member of a gang?" he whispered. "You know she thinks you are the most perfect grandson in the world. She loves you and worships you. She says you look and act just like your mother, her favorite child. How can you do this to Bà?"

"I do it *for* Bà," Sang Le said softly. "I put all the money I make in the dog bank for her house. I tried to get a job, but nobody wants me. I tried to go to school, but nobody helped me. Americans don't like me. Hong doesn't like me, either. She only likes you, Duong. I'm too ugly and skinny for any girl." He snubbed out his cigarette and immediately fished another one from a pack on the table and lit it up.

"Cobra was in re-education camp like me," he continued. "He was in a Hong Kong refugee camp, too. He understands me. He doesn't laugh at me because I don't speak English or because I flunked American school. He knows I play *bida* better than anyone else in town. He is like a big brother."

"But he's a thug!" Danny raised his voice, then quickly lowered it. "He steals and extorts and who knows what else. All the time in the news I hear about somebody getting hurt or killed in Chinatown. You know Cobra and his thugs are behind some of it. What are you going to do when Cobra tells you to smash up Uncle Dao's store downtown? Will you destroy your own family?"

Sang Le shook his head, jetting smoke from his nostrils. "Tho has promised me that he will not harm any member of my family. Don't you see, as long as I am Tho's friend, Uncle Dao is safe."

"You're making a big mistake, cousin. If Bà finds out, she will kick you out of our apartment. I know her."

Sang Le ground the cigarette stub in the ashtray, then sighed. "Please don't tell Bà. I did you a favor by finding Kim. Now, you do me a favor by not telling Bà."

Danny stared at Kim who was laughing and joking with Uncle Dao and Aunt Lien as she gobbled down food. She had been really miserable at the apartment and had been more than ready to come home. Maybe she had learned her lesson. Maybe she had sown her wild oats and would be more obedient now that she knew how much the family loved her.

"Okay, Sang Le, I won't tell Bà this time. But you have to promise me you will try to break away from Cobra before it's too late."

Sang Le nodded and shook Danny's hand. "Okay, cousin, it's a deal."

"What is a deal?" Bà's old voice crackled behind Danny, making him jump.

"Uh . . . uh . . . Sang Le has just promised me he would . . . uh . . . he would . . ."

"Quit smoking," Sang Le quickly blurted out. "I promised him to quit smoking."

Bà picked up the ashtray and crinkled her nose. "Tsh, you promised me you would not smoke anymore, too, but I still smell them on your breath. Promise me again." She removed the cigarette pack from the table and playfully slapped his hand when he tried to take it back.

Sang Le laughed lightly. "Yes, Bà. I promise I will stop smoking."

As she walked away, Sang Le whispered to Danny, "Thank you, cousin, for not telling Bà."

"Okay, but don't forget your promise to me."

Sang Le nodded, then joined his uncles at the table.

Danny was exhausted and could not wait to fall onto his bed, but as he passed by the family altar, he paused and bowed three times. For Kim's safe return, he gave quick thanks to the spirits of his grandfather and great-grandparents, whose photographs sat on the altar. Their eyes, so old and wise-looking, stared down at him. He wondered if he was doing the right thing by not telling anyone about Sang Le and Cobra, but he believed that his cousin was truly sincere and he was determined to give him a chance to prove it.

Danny prayed for strength and wisdom, then crawled into bed. Tomorrow he would see about a make-up history exam. He would ask Mr. Cheng for his job back. And he would try to explain to Tiffany Marie Schultz why he had not spoken to her in nine days. Maybe his life was finally starting to get under control.

Chapter Twelve

Danny couldn't believe his good luck Monday. He had gotten up extra early to hit the history books hard and the teacher let him make up the exam. Even he was surprised how well he had done, considering all the turmoil he had been through the past week.

And Mr. Cheng had welcomed Danny back at the fish market, saying he was short-handed and desperately needed Danny. As for Tiffany Marie, she confronted him on the front steps, her blue eyes riveting him to the wall.

"You're in big trouble, Danny Vo, if you

don't have a good explanation." She jerked the front door open so hard that her hair flew into her eyes.

Danny swallowed hard. He felt lower than a worm as he told Tiffany about Kim running away and explained why he'd missed school the past week. He heard her sigh and saw a wave of relief pass over her face.

"I'm sorry I didn't tell you earlier," Danny apologized. "But I didn't want to bother you with my family's problems. Besides, I thought you were still mad at me for canceling our Easter Sunday plans."

"I was at first. I thought you had backed out because of our stupid argument about Frank. I called you nearly every day last week, but they always said you weren't home. I didn't know what to do, Danny. I was crazy with worry. When you stopped coming to school, I just knew it was my fault." She laughed lightly and tossed her hair back. "I guess that was pretty egotistical of me to think you'd dropped out of school because of me, huh?"

"No . . . not at all." Danny gently pushed a few loose strands of her blond hair back into place. "I guess if you and I ever did break up, maybe I *would* be too depressed to come to school." He smiled and watched her eyes light up and her cheeks turn pink. He took her hand as they slowly walked down the hall.

"Do you remember what you asked me that Friday night we had our little fight?" she asked as she intertwined her fingers with his. "About us having a real date?"

"How could I forget it?"

"Well, I talked to my mom and she agreed to ask for the day shift next Saturday. So, if you still want to, I'm free Saturday night."

Danny couldn't resist leaning over and planting a kiss on her lips, in spite of the fact that Calvin was walking up to join them and Mr. Carnes was standing in the doorway of the history classroom with a disgusted look on his face. It was worth the risk.

Just before lunch, Danny was still glowing with the excitment of Tiffany agreeing to go on a date with him, and his brain was busy planning where he would take her, when Mrs. Kendrick stopped him in the hallway. He knew what the art teacher wanted to talk about even before she spoke.

"Danny, the principal tells me that your cousin Sang Le dropped out of school. I'm so disappointed to hear that. He was an exceptional artist. He could have a great future as an illustrator or commercial artist if he wanted to."

Danny felt his face grow hot. He had not known that Sang Le had officially dropped out. He didn't imagine that his parents or Bà knew about it, either.

"Well, my cousin was having a hard time learning English. He's smart, but he just can't keep up in his classes if he doesn't speak English."

"That's terrible. Maybe he could take English lessons this summer and enroll again next fall. I surely would hate to see his talent wasted."

"Yeah, me too. I'll tell Sang Le you were asking about him."

"Danny, tell Sang Le to come by and see me. The art school downtown is looking for someone for their work-study program. If your cousin would agree to work there—stretch canvas, make frames, and do general cleanup—they will give him free lessons in exchange. It's an opportunity only given to the most exceptional students and those who are rather financially strapped. I took the liberty to show them Sang Le's work, and they agreed to take him. It is a wonderful chance for him to start a career in art."

"That's great, Mrs. Kendrick. I'll tell him as soon as I see him. Maybe he will take English lessons, after all. Thanks."

Danny swirled around, bumping into Hong.

He hardly recognized her with her hair styled into a sleek pageboy and with light makeup on her face. He was amazed how good she looked in blue jeans and a snappy red blouse.

"Sorry," he said and started to walk away. But he paused. "How long were you standing there?"

"A couple of minutes," she said in Vietnamese.

"Did you hear what Mrs. Kendrick said about Sang Le?"

Hong nodded. "Yes."

"How long ago did he drop out of school?"

She glanced at the floor, then drew in a breath. "About a month. He became very disheartened after his last report card. He failed everything except for art and P.E."

"I knew he was doing bad, but I didn't know he had dropped out. Why didn't you tell me, Hong?"

Hong's dark eyes flashed with anger. "Well, if you had ever taken the time to pay attention to your cousin instead of being so involved with Tiffany Schultz, maybe he would have told you about his problems."

Danny ran his fingers through his thick hair. He didn't need this. He started to walk away, then stopped and turned back around.

"Okay," he said. "Maybe I deserved that,

Hong. I was rude to you once. But I never pretended to be anything but a friend to you. You know Sang Le is crazy about you. Why don't you give him a chance? He's not so bad-looking."

"Looks are not everything, Danny Vo. Of course, that is all you boys and men ever think about. It's what's in the heart that counts. I can't help it that my heart feels this way about you. If I had met Sang Le first, perhaps it wouldn't be so."

Danny felt a wave of pity for Hong. She was truly a beautiful girl and maybe if he had not met Tiffany first, he would have felt something for her. He reached out and rested his hand softly on her arm.

"Hong, my cousin loves you. He respects you. If you tell him what Mrs. Kendrick said about working at the art college downtown, maybe he will listen. Maybe you can talk him into taking English lessons and getting his life straightened out. He needs help right now. He's in a lot of trouble. Probably more than you'll ever know."

"Yes, that job would be a wonderful opportunity for Sang Le. I've seen his artwork. It's beautiful. I wish he would listen to Mrs. Kendrick. If only Sang Le would take English lessons more seriously, he could pass all his subjects. It is not easy, but Cuc and I are managing."

Danny saw the bouncy blond hair of Tiffany far down the hall as she hurried to the cafeteria. He should be leaving now or he would get stuck at the end of the lunch line and would miss half his lunch break. Tiffany would worry if he wasn't there.

"Okay, Hong, I'll arrange for Sang Le to call you."

Her eyes lit up. "You will bring Sang Le to my home?"

"Can't you just talk to him on the telephone?"

She shook her head. "It would be better to talk to him in person. On the phone, he might hang up on me if he doesn't want to listen. Can you come over this Saturday?"

Danny glanced down the hall. His date with Tiffany was that Saturday.

"Can you make it Friday or Sunday? I have to do something Saturday."

Hong saw Danny's gaze focused on Tiffany. Her eyes grew moist.

"As you wish," she said softly and hung her head in defeat. "Any day will be agreeable with me. I am home every night." She turned, then added in words so soft they were barely audible. "You do not have to accompany Sang Le," she said, then hurried down the hall on silent feet.

Danny groaned and clenched his fists. He had not intended to hurt her feelings again, but it was too late.

"Thanks, Hong," he called out to her back. "I'll tell Sang Le tonight."

Danny kept his promise and waited up for his cousin. He only felt slightly dishonest when he told Sang Le that Hong wanted to see him and had invited him to her house. Sang Le began walking the floor, one minute grinning and giggling, the next tugging at his hair and pacing like a nervous tiger. Danny did not tell him about the conversation with Mrs. Kendrick. He decided it would be better if the news came from the lips of Hong.

The meeting was arranged for Tuesday, and Sang Le could have been a groom on his wedding day for all the worrying about clothes and cologne and shoes and how to comb his hair. When he finished, Danny had to admit that his cousin didn't look half bad.

Danny spent a restless night sitting at his desk, wondering how Sang Le would feel when he found out that the meeting with Hong had an ulterior motive. He half expected his cousin to burst through the room, his hands clenched into fists and his eyes flashing with anger. But no such thing happened. Sang Le opened the door so softly, Danny didn't know he was in the room at first.

"Cousin Duong," he said softly.

"Hey, Sang Le. How did it go with the girl of your dreams?" Danny twisted his desk chair around.

"It was wonderful. I thought Hong did not care for me at all, but she really does. She gave me a message from Mrs. Kendrick about a job at the art school downtown. And she encouraged me to take English lessons and return to school. She is a truly beautiful girl. I love her more than ever now."

Danny sighed with relief and smiled. He slapped Sang Le on the back.

"That's great news. So, are you going to take the job?"

"I want to very much. But there is no money in it, only free art lessons. I must have money for your family's house. I must repay all of you for bringing me to America." Sang Le sat on the windowsill and blew cigarette smoke out into the night air. True to his promise, he was down to only two smokes a day.

"But if you take lessons and become a commercial artist, you can pay us back when you get a job. The important thing is to learn English and get a high school diploma."

"Yes, that is exactly what Hong said."

"Does she know about Cobra?"

"If you mean my friend Nguyen Tho, she knows nothing about him. Please, cousin, do not tell her. She thinks I work at the rice bag factory at night. I told her I dropped out of school because I work ten hours a night. She truly believes me. Please, cousin, it would destroy her to know I lied."

"Okay, okay. I won't tell her. But you have to promise me to get out of Cobra's gang. You're not like him and his creeps. They don't want to work, they want easy money. They're mixed up with the murders near Vietnam Plaza, aren't they?"

"I have never killed anyone, you must believe me."

"Why don't you just break away and go back to school? It's almost May. We've only got about one month of school left. I know you can do it, with Hong's help. Just forget about Cobra and his gang."

Sang Le heaved a long, ragged sigh. "I would like to, but it is impossible. I have become too useful to Tho. He does not want me to leave now. I know too much. I saw something once . . . something terrible." His words trailed off to a whisper and his large liquid eyes stared out the window into the empty night.

"It's better to leave them now while you can," Danny pleaded. "Later, it will be too late."

"It is already too late."

"No, Sang Le. You have to try. Start slowly. Miss one or two nights. Tell him you're sick. Keep away from the *bida* hall. He'll get the idea."

Sang Le snorted and tossed the cigarette butt into the courtyard. "Yes, he will most certainly get the idea. All right, cousin, I will try. Starting tomorrow, I will begin my new life."

In spite of his good intentions, Sang Le did not quit Cobra's gang. If anything, he was plunged in even deeper than before. Every day for the rest of the week, Sang Le was out very late. Wednesday night he screamed savagely in his sleep, shouting out strange names as he thrashed against an invisible foe. Thursday night he did not come home at all.

Danny felt disappointed and helpless. He had been so sure that Hong would be able to persuade his cousin to change his lifestyle. Of all the people Sang Le knew, Hong was the one he respected and loved the most, next to Bà, of course. Danny toyed with the idea of telling Bà but dismissed it. The old woman's heart would surely break if she found out that her perfect grandson was in a vicious gang, the very gang that had been harassing her youngest son at his downtown store.

Friday night Danny came in from the fish market, showered, and dropped into bed. He was too tired to do anything else. Tomorrow was the night of his big date with Tiffany, the first one they would ever have alone. He had made arrangements to work the morning shift in the fish market so he could wash his mother's car and get cleaned up and dressed for Saturday night. And most important of all, he had decided to buy Tiffany a friendship ring, a tiny heart-shaped ruby in a delicate gold band. It would cost him two weeks' pay and he was guessing at her finger size. He would have to get up at five in the morning for the early shift, but it would be worth it.

It was early May now and the weather was already hot. As usual, the air conditioner was turned off to save on the electric bill. The soft hum of a rotary fan lulled Danny into a fast, deep sleep.

In the early morning, a loud thud woke him up. He saw his cousin staggering in as he had done for many months.

"What happened to you last night?" Danny mumbled, his eyes only half open.

"I had business to take care of. I couldn't get away until morning, so it was pointless to come home. Did anyone ask about me?"

Danny sat up and rubbed his eyes. It was four-thirty, almost time for him to get up.

"No, I guess they thought you had to work extra late," Danny said. Suddenly he heard a soft rapping on the door.

Sang Le opened it.

"Bà!" Sang Le stepped back.

The small woman grabbed his arm with one hand and with the other thrashed his legs with a slender bamboo switch.

"Go away, bad spirits!" she hissed.

"Bà?" Danny leaped out of the bed and jerked on his long-tailed shirt. "What are you doing?"

"I am driving those bad devils out of my grandson. They make him do evil things."

Sang Le crumpled to his knees, not resisting but bowing his head and receiving each blow in silence. Tears welled in his eyes, then spilled down his cheeks.

Danny grabbed the old woman's frail hand and forced her to stop. He was amazed at the strength in her tiny body.

"Bà, you're crazy. Sang Le doesn't have any evil spirits in him."

"No, no, leave her alone," Sang Le sobbed. "She is right, cousin. Let her drive them away."

Danny took the switch and tossed it out the window.

"I know you belong to that bad *toan du dang*," she said in a high, shrill voice that ended on a whine. "You think I don't notice you stay out late. Uncle Dao saw you with those bad boys that threatened him. How could you join a *toan du dang*? Why? Didn't your dear mother teach you better? You bring shame on the whole family."

Sang Le sniffed and pawed at his shirt pocket. He pulled out a crumpled wad of money. "Bà, I did it for you. For the house you want so bad." He got up and dashed into the hall, returning with the plaster-of-Paris dog bank. He shoved the money inside the dog's head. "See, Bà, for you and the family. You brought me to America, I have to pay you back."

The hard glint in Bà's eyes never softened as she grabbed the dog and smashed it against the wall. It shattered into pieces and money spilled to the floor. She seized a handful and shook it in Sang Le's face.

"This is bad money. This money belongs to evil spirits. I would rather die than live in a house bought with this wicked money. I will burn it all tomorrow and pray for your soul to come back."

Tears flowed down Sang Le's face and spilled on the floor as he dropped to his knees and hung his head.

"Bà, forgive me," he sobbed.

"It is not for me to forgive. Your mother and Duong's mother can tell you about gangs. In Da Nang a gang of wicked boys attacked them. They raped your mother and Duong's mother. I don't want this gang money." She spat on the bills in her hand and threw them to the floor.

Danny felt his face go pale. Never had he heard anyone say that his own mother had been gang-raped in Da Nang. Suddenly he understood why she was so frightened when she saw him speaking to Cobra at the market. He swallowed hard and fought the urge to cry alongside Sang Le.

"Your mother sacrificed everything for you," Bà continued. "She worked hard at the lacquer factory to save money to try to get your father out of re-education camp. She stayed in Vietnam when she could have come to America with us, because you were sick. She signed bad papers to get you medicine. She killed herself because you had to go to jail. She died for you. How would your mother feel if she knew you were in a gang of bad boys? She hated gangs so much. I pray her spirit does not look down on us tonight."

Sang Le sobbed shamelessly. He grabbed Bà's ankles and kissed her old feet. For several minutes he cried, then Bà gently touched his chin and forced him to look up.

"I only did it for the money, Bà. For the house."

"Money is nothing, child. Honor and respect are everything. Without honor, all the money in the world is worth no more than a bag of stones. Always remember who you are. You have the blood of a dragon flowing in your veins. You must act with honor and bravery like a dragon. You must sacrifice for the good of your family. Now, tell me child, what are you going to do?"

Thuy, who had awakened from the noise, handed Sang Le a roll of toilet tissue. Sang Le tore off a section and blew his nose.

"I promise to leave the gang, Bà. I will never take another cent from them. I will take the money back."

"Good. And you will return to school and learn English?"

"Is there nothing you do not know, Bà?" Sang Le said, amazed.

The old woman's eyes glistened as she glanced at Danny. "I only know what I am supposed to know." She turned and left as silently as she had come, closing the door behind her.

Sang Le refused to sleep in his bed, saying he did not deserve any human comforts that night. A few minutes later, Danny heard Thuy's heavy breathing and knew his little brother was asleep. Then he heard Sang Le's slow, even breath and slight snore. Danny lay awake, waiting for the usual crying and screaming and tossing that tormented his cousin every night. But that night Sang Le slept peacefully.

Chapter Thirteen

The band was playing a slow tune. Danny pulled Tiffany nearer and closed his eyes as he breathed in her soft perfume. They swayed gently as the music floated over the potted palms lining the dance floor. The lead singer's words sank into Danny's heart, and every line seemed to be written just for him and Tiffany.

If the world should end tomorrow
I would feel no pain or sorrow
For I have known heaven in your arms tonight.

They returned from the tiny dance floor to their table, a cozy one in a dark corner of the exclusive restaurant. "This is great," she said as she slipped her hand into his and smiled.

"Yeah, I want to kick myself when I think of all the times over the past two years I could have asked you out." Danny stirred the ice cubes in his glass of tea. "But it'll be different next year, right? We'll have a lot of things to do—football games, field trips, the junior prom." He squeezed her hand.

Tiffany sighed. "Juniors already. And after that seniors. Are you going to college, Danny?"

"I'll be trying to earn a scholarship. That's why I have to crack down on my studying for the next two years. No more goofing off. I barely passed history."

"But you had a lot of family problems. Nobody can blame you for being too upset to study with your little sister missing and with your cousin needing your help. Next year will be great. Everything will be perfect."

Danny leaned over and placed a soft kiss on Tiffany's petal-smooth cheek. "You're beautiful, Tiffany. Inside and out," he said. Danny removed a small black velvet box from his jacket pocket and flipped the lid open. A tiny ruby winked in the candlelight like red wine.

"Oh, it's beautiful, Danny," she whispered and slipped the ring onto her finger. It was too big.

"Uh, sorry," Danny said as he ran his fingers through his hair. "I told the jeweler I might have to bring it back for a different size."

"That's okay. I can wrap tape around it or something."

"No, no, let me return it for the right size." He replaced the ring and slid it into his pants pocket.

"Oh, Danny, I'm so happy tonight." She leaned over and kissed his lips tenderly.

They danced two more times, then left. They drove around and talked a little while longer. The time flew by, and Danny felt a stab of pain when he glanced at his watch and saw that it was time to take Tiffany home.

They sat in Tiffany's driveway a few moments for a final kiss, then Danny walked her to her front door. They heard the TV and through the picture window Danny saw Bradley's wheelchair, and Tiffany's mom asleep on the sofa. He felt sorry for Tiffany, having to always take care of her brother. But in a way, he thought, she must be a better person because of the experience. She was kind, caring, and slow to lose her temper.

"Good night," she said softly. "I had a great time. Thanks for everything."

"I had a great time, too. I'll call you to-morrow."

Danny leaned his head down and kissed Tiffany's lips one last time. His heart beat faster and his arms did not want to let her go. She felt so warm and alive.

Blaring headlights suddenly streaked across the front porch. Danny felt Tiffany stiffen and pull away from him. He held a hand over his eyes to shade out the bright beams coming from the driveway.

"It's Frank and Brian," Tiffany whispered. Danny felt her arms start to tremble. "I've got to go."

"No, wait," Danny said as he grabbed her arm. "It's time we faced your brother and told him the truth. We can't keep running away every time we see him."

"You don't know my brother. He does everything that jerk Brian tells him to," Tiffany said, trying to pull free. "Go now, Danny, before it's too late. *Please*."

Danny let go of Tiffany's arm. He had seen that look before, the same look of terror his mother had in her eyes the day she talked about the gangs of Da Nang.

"Okay, you go inside," he whispered. "I'll handle this."

"No, don't even try to talk to him. Just run to your car, please."

"I'm not running from anyone," Danny snapped back.

"Hey, get away from my sister!" Frank Schultz's angry voice boomed across the lawn. "Tiffany Marie, get inside. I'll take care of you later."

Tiffany pressed her body against the front door as if frozen in a trance.

Three teenage boys and a man in his early twenties scrambled out of the red Mustang convertible, not bothering to open the doors. Their heavy steel-toed boots clomped on the sidewalk and their long, dull-colored raincoats swished. With their shaved heads and sullen faces, they looked like zombies from a horror movie. Large black pupils glowed in the middle of Frank's bright blue eyes, the same blue as Tiffany's.

"What do you think you're doing on my porch, chink?" he demanded and swung a golf iron at a clump of flowers in the entryway. Red roses spewed across the sidewalk.

"That'll be your head next, gook," the oldest one said. "Let's get him, Frank. Let's teach him a lesson for messing around with our white women." Danny smelled the pungent odor of beer on his breath.

Frank grabbed Danny's arm and jerked him off the porch. Danny thought that the pudgy teenager would be weak and soft, but the strength in his arms knocked Danny off balance. He stumbled into the yard and landed on his knees.

"Leave him alone," Tiffany screeched. She darted to Danny's side and helped him stand up.

"Hey you guys, be cool," Danny said, brushing the grass off the new black jacket and expensive white shirt that he had borrowed from Calvin for the date. He could imagine what Cal would say if anything happened to his favorite clothes. "We just went to a fancy restaurant to eat. Nothing happened."

"Hey, Frank, you mean you're letting your sister date a gook?" the oldest boy said and laughed a whiny laugh.

Frank's eyes narrowed and his lips turned down in rage as he rushed forward and grabbed Danny's collar. With the force of his bulk, he shoved Danny against his mother's car in the driveway. Tiffany stood in the middle of the yard, her hands over her mouth in terror.

"Don't you ever come near my sister again, chink, or you're a dead man. We don't want your kind. Why don't you go back to your rice paddies and jungles where you belong. If it wasn't for gooks like you, Americans wouldn't have died. Isn't that right, Brian?"

The oldest one nodded. "Yeah, you remember what I taught you very well, Frank. These chinks are the ones getting all the good jobs. They're teachers' pets. Your science project was as good as theirs, wasn't that what you told me? You didn't win just because *they* get special favors. Right, Frank?"

Frank nodded. His blue eyes burned with hatred. "Go back to Vietnam, you stinking Vietcong pig."

Danny felt the blood surging through his veins and pounding in his ears. How could anyone be so stupid as to think he was a Vietcong communist? His family had left Vietnam to get away from the communist dictators. At every party, or family celebration, his father and uncle and their friends wept for the loss of their country and plotted how to get Vietnam out of the hands of communists.

"I don't want to fight you Nazis," Danny said. He pushed Frank away and walked toward Tiffany.

"Hey, Frank, he called you a Nazi," Brian taunted. "I think he meant it as an insult. Are you going to let him get away with that?"

The large, clumsy teenager gritted his teeth

and grabbed Danny's shirt. The sound of ripping cloth filled the night air. Danny felt sick as he glanced down at Cal's new white shirt. That was going to cost him at least thirty bucks.

"You didn't have to ruin my shirt. All of you are nothing but a bunch of stupid gorillas. Get out of my way."

Danny started swinging and smashed his fist into Frank's jaw. The big hulk tried to grab Danny, but Danny was lighter on his feet and quicker. He dodged and dropped a kick on Frank's thigh.

"Oooh, I'm really scared," Brian heckled. "He knows karate. He's Bruce Lee in disguise. Oh, please, kung fu master, don't hurt me." As he dropped to his knees, Brian made a baby face and pretended to weep. Danny fought the urge to kick his face.

The two older boys started laughing hysterically.

"Shut up," Brian suddenly snapped and climbed to his feet. "Jason, go get the baseball bat. We're going to have to teach this piece of trash a lesson."

Tiffany ran forward and tugged on Brian's arm.

"Leave him alone, Brian. He didn't do anything. He's my friend."

"Frank, get this tramp away from me."

Frank grabbed her arm and twisted it behind her back. Danny ran forward and tried to break his grasp. But it was a bad mistake. Brian grabbed Danny from behind and held his arms tightly.

"Do it, Frank," Brian urged. "Teach him to keep away from our white women."

Frank glanced at his sister's weeping face.

"Go ahead. What are you waiting for, your mama?" Brian hissed.

With a scream, Frank began punching. Pain shot through Danny's stomach and chest. He wanted to throw up, and he fought to fill his lungs with air. He felt the blood drain from his face.

"No!" Tiffany screamed again. "Please! Please, let him go."

"We're not through having fun, little sis," Brian said. "I don't think he's learned his lesson yet. Do you, Frank?"

Frank didn't speak; he continued pounding Danny's stomach and face until blood spilled from his nose down the front of Calvin's new shirt.

"Please," Tiffany wailed and pulled at Frank's hands, trying to force herself between Danny and Frank. "I promise to never speak to him again. I'll never see him. I promise. Please," she sobbed. Through his watery eyes, Danny could hardly see her face.

The front door opened and Mrs. Schultz stood in her bare feet and housecoat, her eyes puffy from lack of sleep.

"What is going on here?" she grumbled. Then she saw Danny. "My God, what are you doing! Franklin Schultz, stop it!"

"Uh-oh—Mama's mad," Brian taunted.

"Go back inside, Mom. This is none of your business." Frank hit Danny again, and Brian cackled in glee.

"Look at you. You're just like your father," the woman shouted. "Always getting into fights. Always thinking you know better than anyone else."

"No, I am *not* like him!"

"Ha! You are his spitting image right now."

Frank held his fist in the air, poised to strike one more blow. Rage burned in his eyes for several seconds before he swallowed hard and stepped back.

"Let him go, Brian," Frank said between gritted teeth. "The little baby can't take any more, anyhow."

Danny felt the hands behind him slowly loosen their grip. Tiffany and her mother hurried to him, but he pushed them back and climbed to his feet. His shaking legs fought to keep their balance as he staggered to his car and slid inside. He jerked the jacket off and wiped it across his eyes so he could see the ignition.

Danny felt tears of shame streaming down his face as he drove down the street. He didn't have to look at the street signs; he had been this way so many times, he knew it by heart.

When he pulled into the apartment parking lot, it was after midnight. He was grateful that no lights were on inside. He eased his body through the front door, tiptoed across the living room, and entered the bathroom. He threw up again and again, then washed his face and took a hot shower. He stared at the bloody rag that was Calvin's favorite shirt. He didn't know how he was going to explain it, but at the moment that was the least of his worries. He put a Band-Aid on his chin and stared at his bruised and cut face. It could have been a lot worse. Frank had been holding back, and the guy with the baseball bat had never taken a swing at him. He guessed he owed his life to Tiffany and her mother's interference. Somehow that thought made him feel even worse.

Danny snuck into his bedroom, closing the door softly behind him. Thuy was fast asleep in the bunk bed. Sang Le, true to his promise to Bà, was home, too. He rolled over and sat up, rubbing his eyes.

"How did your date go?" he whispered.

"Okay," Danny replied in a hoarse voice. He quickly cleared his throat. "It was great." A line of pain shot through his jaw as he spoke. He gently rubbed it while he was in the closet getting his pajamas.

"Is something wrong?" Sang Le asked.

"No, no. It was great, really."

Danny heard the click of the lamp and gritted his teeth. He scoured his brain for what he would say when his cousin saw his pummeled face. He would have to make up a good story and stick to it with the rest of the family, too. Slowly Danny turned around and stepped into the light. Sang Le gasped.

"Cousin, what happened?"

"I fell down a rocky hill and got all scraped up. I was acting crazy, dancing in the moonlight on top of a rock wall. Fell right off and felt like a real fool."

Sang Le threw back his covers and walked closer. He cocked his head to one side and studied Danny's face.

"You've been fighting, little cousin. Who beat you like that?"

Danny pushed his cousin aside. "You're crazy, man. I told you I fell off a rock wall. Now, leave me alone and let me get some sleep."

Danny flipped the lamp switch off, then crawled under the covers. He heard the mattress squeak as Sang Le returned to bed. For a long time, no sound filled the room except for Thuy's regular breathing. Pain throbbed in Danny's face and stomach. He thought about getting an aspirin but didn't want to get up.

"Cousin Duong, tell me who hurt you. It must have been more than one person. Tell me who they were, please. You know I will find out anyway."

Danny sighed. "It was a bunch of skinheads."

"The boys with no hair on top?"

"Yeah. They hate anybody who isn't white. They harass blacks, Hispanics, Asians. They go around beating people up with baseball bats. Tiffany's brother Frank belongs to one of their gangs. He got mad because I was dating Tiffany."

Sang Le remained quiet a long time, then laughed lightly.

"They are nothing, little cousin. My friend Cobra can take care of them like that." The sound of a crisp snap filled the air. "They are mere children compared to Cobra. Don't worry, we will take care of them."

"No!" Danny bolted up from the bed and flipped on the light. The glare sent a shock wave of pain through his eyes and head. "No, Sang Le. Stay out of it. Don't tell Cobra about this; it's none of his business. The last thing I need is to be caught in the middle of a gang war."

"But your honor, Danny. They have ruined your honor."

"I'll get even with Frank Schultz. But let me do it my way. Besides, you promised Bà that you wouldn't have anything to do with Cobra's gang from now on. Have you decided to go back on your word so soon?"

Sang Le sighed and laid back down. "I will stay out of it. It is your battle. But if you need my help, I am always here. I will save your skin again, like I did the time you fell into the lotus moat, little cousin, if you want me to."

Danny saw Sang Le's hand reaching across the narrow space between their beds.

"Okay, cousin," Danny said as they clasped hands. "It's a deal. If I need your help, I will let you know."

Chapter Fourteen

Danny slapped a wad of money into Calvin's opened palm after they settled into their seats behind the physics lab table.

"That's the last I owe you for the shirt and jacket," Danny said, "so I don't want to hear you moaning and groaning anymore."

"I ought to charge you interest, too, man. It took me three weekends to pick out that jacket." Calvin opened his wallet and stuffed the money inside. "Oh, well—guess you paid extra out of your skin, huh?"

"Yeah, no fooling." Danny rubbed his jaw and chin. The bruises were almost gone, but one of the cuts had left a thin white scar below his chin. "Have you seen Tiffany today?"

"I saw her at the water fountain five minutes ago, but you know she'll take off like a scared rabbit if she sees you. Face it, man, that girl's history. She doesn't want to have anything to do with you anymore. Not if she wants to live a little longer."

Danny sighed. Calvin was right. For the past week, since their ill-fated date, she had kept her promise to her brother. She had not spoken to or sat near Danny. She wouldn't even look at him.

Seeing him beaten up before her eyes must have changed her life, Danny thought. She no longer laughed with her friends or smiled at everyone she met. She kept her head low as she walked from one class to the other, glancing up only briefly, as if watching for something or someone. Whether it was him or Frank Schultz, Danny didn't know.

Danny's attempts at communication with Tiffany had been miserable failures all week. She refused to answer the phone at her house, or hung up on him if she did. In the mornings she dashed from the bus to the girls' rest room and lingered there until only seconds before the first bell rang, then she slipped inside and sat in the first row under the teacher's nose, instead of in the back where Danny usually sat. The notes he tagged to her locker were returned to him unread. At lunch, she vanished entirely. Danny had not figured out yet where she went, though Calvin said he thought he saw her going into the gymnasium once.

"I tried waiting for her at her locker," Danny said, "but she never goes to it anymore. I don't now how she's managing to study. She never seems to change books."

"Ah, she probably has her locker mate do it for her. She's pretty smart, you know."

"Sometimes I wonder about that," Danny grumbled. He flipped open his physics lab book and tried to concentrate on the experiment instructions.

"What do you mean?"

"I guess I mean she really acts dumb when it comes to her brother. He's a menace to society. Why doesn't she tell somebody about him?"

"Who should she tell? Her mom? The police?"

"No, her mom knows about Frank. She just pretends nothing is wrong."

"Maybe you should turn Frank Schultz in to the cops, Danny. He beat you up pretty bad. At least tell the principal and get the creep suspended."

"That would probably make things worse for Tiffany. You know, sometimes I think Frank isn't entirely to blame. It was the older guy, Brian, who was calling the shots. He was the one that kept egging Frank on. I think if Frank and I could just sit down and talk for a while, maybe we could be friends."

"Say what!" Calvin cocked his head to one side. "Now you *are* talking like a fool, man. That Frank Schultz doesn't want any friends in this school. He'd probably be glad to be kicked out. I hear he's flunking everything but P.E. He'd probably thank you for getting him suspended."

Danny smiled. "No, I don't think so."

After class, Danny waited for Tiffany, but as usual she did not appear at her locker, so Danny reluctantly climbed into the bus with Calvin. Out the window he saw a red Mustang pull up to the curb. As she had been doing ever since their date, Tiffany hurried to the red car and climbed in, her face expressionless. Danny watched the Mustang pull away in a cloud of billowy exhaust fumes and with squealing tires. He saw Tiffany's head tilt upward toward the bus. He waved and thought he saw her head nod, only slightly. But it might have been his imagination.

Danny leaned back into the seat. He closed his eyes and thought of the last time he had held

Tiffany—the softness of her silky dress on his fingers, the smell of her perfume, the warmth of her body next to his while they danced to the slow music. The words to the song returned to him night and day:

If the world should end tomorrow
I would feel no pain or sorrow
For I have known Heaven in your arms tonight.

The song had been no more than a pleasant, romantic dance tune to him a week ago. Now the words haunted him. That night in her arms should have been the beginning of their love, not the end.

"Do you have to work tonight?" Calvin's words broke into Danny's daydream. He opened his eyes and saw that they had already arrived at the bus stop near his apartment complex. He straightened up and pulled his book satchel from the floor.

"No. I arranged to work a double shift tomorrow. I had thought maybe I'd be able to talk Tiffany into another date by tonight. Guess I was wrong." He stood and waited for the bus to come to a complete stop.

Calvin shook his head sympathetically and put a hand on Danny's back. "Man, you're not fit for anything in this condition. You've got to forget that girl. Why don't we go out for pizza and some video games? It just so happens I've got a wallet full of money. Let me treat." He grinned and patted his back pocket.

Danny searched his friend's face a long time. "Sorry, Cal, but I don't feel like having fun. Think I'll take a bath and go to bed. I'm so sleepy I can't keep my eyes open. I'll call you later. Maybe we can do something Sunday."

"Okay, man. Take it easy. No girl is worth all that pain, you know."

Danny forced a smile and waved good-bye to his friend. What he had said to Cal was true. He had been fighting a deep sense of weariness all day. He had been getting the same amount of sleep as usual, but life had nothing interesting to offer without Tiffany. She had been his reason for getting up every day for the past three years.

As Danny started up the concrete stairs, its rails now half covered by Bà's bitter melon vine, he saw a strange car pull into the parking lot. Sang Le climbed out, holding a painting under one arm. Danny waited for his cousin to catch up.

"Who was that?" Danny asked.

"Mrs. Kendrick. She took me to the downtown art school today. See, they showed me how to build frames. They let me keep this one." He held up a watercolor of Hong. A striking bamboo frame surrounded it, emphasizing the delicate colors and sense of serenity.

"You took the job?"

"Yes. I am going to take English lessons all summer. Mrs. Kendrick said she will help me. And I will return to school in the fall. I know I will pass my subjects once I understand English better."

"That's great." Danny slapped his cousin's back. "I knew you could do it if you just got away from Cobra."

Sang Le's smile dropped a moment and he grew silent. Danny crinkled his eyebrows and tilted his head to one side.

"You haven't seen Cobra lately, have you? You know you promised Bà you'd drop out of that gang."

"Oh, I have dropped out of the gang. I only saw Cobra one time this week. I told him about Bà and I gave him back all the money."

"What did he say?"

"In a way Tho was most understanding, but . . ."

"But what?"

"Nothing."

"No, tell me. What did Cobra say? Did he threaten you?"

"Not exactly, but he predicts I will come back. He says I will not be able to stay away from his friendship because we are too much alike. He says he will be waiting for me tonight at Ho's *bida* hall. It is so tempting to go back. I feel terrible that Bà has no money in the dog bank now. Your parents are just as far removed from buying their house as when I arrived. I have done nothing to repay them."

"Well, you're not going back to Cobra, cousin. I won't let you out of my sight tonight. I've got great plans for us." Danny put his arm around Sang Le's thin shoulders and they climbed the stairs together.

Bà was watching volume number fifteen of the twenty-volume set of Vietnamese video-tapes—a long, heartrending story of peasant girls and kung fu and an evil wizard who could change his shape into any animal. Like all the movies they rented, this one had been made in China with Chinese actors and actresses. Vietnamese had been dubbed over their words, making the lips out of sync. One translator played the role of many men, hopelessly trying to disguise his voice for each different character. At times it was comical, even though the women were weeping and the men were pulling their hair and beating their chests in a touching death scene. Bà, as usual, sat in her favorite big chair, her eyes glued to the TV screen.

Sang Le leaned over and placed a kiss on

Bà's gray bun. She patted his hand without taking her eyes from the television.

After raiding the refrigerator and watching the end of the videotape, Danny and Sang Le retired to their room. Thuy was spending the night with a friend, so they had the bedroom to themselves.

"What do you want to do, Sang Le? Paint a picture?"

"My paintbrush is ruined. Dao's baby girl stuck it in some oil paint and it dried hard. I haven't had time to buy another one. Perhaps I should go out and buy one now."

"No way. You're staying right here tonight. The nearest place to buy a paintbrush is a mile away."

"Okay, I'll do it tomorrow." He stared around the room, as if trying to find something that would interest him more than going to the *bida* hall. Danny felt the urgency, too. He opened a desk drawer and pulled out some playing cards and began shuffling them Vietnamese style, quickly slapping them hand over hand.

"How about a game of *sap sam*?" Danny asked. "I know it's like playing poker with thirteen cards, but I get confused with the rules sometimes. You can teach me everything you know."

Sang Le chuckled. "That would take a long time, little cousin. *Sap sam* is no fun with only two people playing. And without betting money, it is useless."

"I've got two dollars." Danny removed his wallet and laid out the money and emptied his pockets of change.

Sang Le laughed louder. "That is the most pitiful amount to play for I have ever seen."

"Okay, then let's play *cac-te*. Can't two people play that?"

Sang Le nodded and took the cards from Danny. He shuffled them rapidly, slapping them hand over hand, then dealt out six cards to himself and to Danny.

They ate snacks and played cards. It was a stifling hot night. Beads of sweat trickled down their temples and shirtless backs. Danny was fighting off sleep but forced himself to stay awake. It would be the first Friday that Sang Le had stayed away from Cobra. Danny imagined the slim, nervous man in the black leather jacket. He would be pacing in front of the *bida* hall, or sitting inside, sipping a glass of iced coffee or beer and pretending to not notice that Sang Le was not there.

Just before midnight Danny got up to get another Coke. He noticed that Bà had fallen asleep in front of the television. A talk show was blaring and the guest was a pretty blond actress. She wore her hair the same way as Tiffany. A sudden jolt of pain ran through Danny's chest. He had not thought of Tiffany for several hours. He had been so busy trying to keep Sang Le home that he had forgotten his own problems.

When he returned to the bedroom, his cousin was rummaging through his pants and shirts and opening and closing drawers.

"What're you looking for? More money to pay me? Don't worry, I'll take your IOU." Danny grabbed a towel and popped his cousin's legs.

"Ha! You only had beginner's luck. You are the one who will owe me soon. I am looking for cigarettes. I can't play well without a cigarette in my mouth."

Danny laughed. "So that's your problem. And I thought it was because I'm such a fast learner. Didn't you promise Bà you wouldn't smoke anymore?"

"Yes, I know. But it is so hard to quit. I only smoke two times a day now. I haven't smoked for five hours. Only one cigarette and I will be okay."

"Well, we don't have any here in the house. Cha gave them up last year. The company he works for made all the workers stop smoking."

"Then I have to go buy some." Sang Le reached into the pile of dollar bills and loose change lying on the floor beside the cards. He stuffed three dollars into his pants pocket, then slipped on a clean shirt. "I will be back in about ten minutes."

"Where are you going?" Danny rose to his feet.

"Tilson's Grocery Store is only a block away."

"Sang Le, you promised me you wouldn't go out tonight."

"It is only for cigarettes. I promise you, little cousin. What can I do with only three dollars in my pocket?" He flashed a grin.

Danny forced a smile. "Okay, then. I'll come with you."

Sang Le shook his head. "No, I have to prove to you that I am telling the truth. I must overcome this temptation alone."

Danny nodded. It did make sense.

"All right, then. I'll see you in ten minutes. Buy a bag of popcorn, too." Danny picked up a dollar from his pile and pushed it into Sang Le's shirt pocket. He watched his cousin slip on his shoes on the front porch, then lightly bound down the steps into the hot, humid night.

Danny sat at the desk. He studied the latest drawing Sang Le had been working on. As he turned it over, he noticed a piece of scrap paper neatly folded over several times. He unfolded it and saw his cousin's small, neat handwriting. It was a love poem to Hong, full of passion. Danny felt embarrassed to see how the English words were so badly misspelled. He thought about correcting them but he knew he would hurt Sang Le's feelings.

He opened the desk drawer to drop it inside and saw more sheets of notebook paper covered with the same small, tight writing. Danny read each one. Most of them had been written in Vietnamese first, and then a word-by-word translation attempted. Danny could not read Vietnamese, but he imagined that the words were more lyrical and beautiful than the choppy English. Sang Le had obviously struggled for hours over each one because he had crossed out the English words again and again, and had erased until some parts of the sheets had holes rubbed in them.

By the time Danny had finished reading all the poems, he realized that more time had passed than he had intended. Sang Le had left around midnight. It was already half past twelve. A strange feeling crept over Danny and he shivered.

Maybe his cousin had to wait in line. Maybe Tilson's was closed and he'd decided to walk the four blocks to the Asian market.

Danny stood and began pacing. He pulled back the curtain on the bedroom window and scanned the parking lot below. Sang Le would have to walk right under the window to get inside. Danny pulled up a chair and sat down. As usual, the air conditioner was turned off to save electricity and the window was open. Moths and bugs thrashed around the lamp in the court-yard and swallows dived at them. Beneath the street lamp a toad silently, patiently awaited its prey.

Danny crept to the front door. His grand-mother had turned off the TV and was asleep on the sofa. As he slipped into a pair of thongs on the front porch, Danny stopped. He had told Sang Le he trusted him. If he went looking for his cousin now and met him on the way, Danny would feel awful. Sang Le's feelings would be hurt and their relationship damaged. Quietly, Danny removed the thongs and returned to his bedroom. He would give Sang Le another fifteen minutes. Then he would walk to Tilson's store, and if his cousin wasn't there, on to the *bida* hall near the old Chinese movie house.

Danny played a game of solitaire, then

glanced at the telephone. He wondered if Tiffany was still awake. Her mother usually worked on Friday nights, and Frank was never home on weekends. Bradley probably couldn't answer the phone, so that left only Tiffany. Danny's heart began to pound at the thought of hearing her voice, even if she just said hello then hung up. His fingers trembled as he picked up the receiver. He dialed her number, then held his breath.

"Hello," a boy's voice said.

Danny was speechless for a moment. He had never expected Bradley to answer.

"Is Tiffany home?" he finally asked.

"No, she went out a while ago."

"Bradley, this is Danny. Is she really out or did she tell you to say that?"

"Honest, Danny. She's out with Susan and Julie. They went to the movies and I think she's going to spend the night at Julie's house."

"Julie Martin?"

"Yeah."

Danny's heart skipped. Julie Martin lived in a house about two blocks from his apartment. It was a nice neighborhood, separated from the apartments by a small bayou. Danny could easily walk to Julie's, knock on the door, and ask to see Tiffany. Maybe she would talk to him if she felt safe from her brother.

"Thanks, Bradley."

"Uh, Danny . . . do you know Julie's phone number?"

"I can look it up in the phone book. I know what street she lives on. Why, is something wrong?"

"Umm, kind of. My brother Frank was supposed to stay home with me tonight so Tiffany could go out. But he left a little while ago with Brian. I don't know when he's coming back. It's not important, but . . . I've got to, you know . . . use the bathroom. I can wait a little while longer, but if he's not back soon I'm going to wet my britches. Mom will be really mad."

"Don't worry, Brad. I'll call Julie's house and talk to Tiffany."

Danny hung up and charged into the hall for the residential phone book. He couldn't believe how many Martins there were listed, but only one lived on Triola Street. He hummed a song as he dialed. Never had he expected to have such a good excuse for calling her. Tiffany was devoted to Bradley and would be so thankful to Danny. Maybe it would be the icebreaker he had been looking for.

But the phone was busy. Danny cursed under his breath and dialed again. He waited two minutes, which seemed more like thirty, then tried again. Still the line was busy. He slammed the receiver down and quickly changed into his best blue jeans and a clean shirt and socks. He tied his sneakers, then removed the friendship ring from his desk drawer and slipped it into his pants pocket. He had returned it to the jewelers and exchanged it for a smaller size, but had not been able to give it to Tiffany.

Danny dialed Julie Martin's number one more time. It was still busy.

"Well, at least I have a real excuse for going over there," he said aloud. He scribbled a note for Sang Le and left it on the middle of the bed, then tiptoed to the front door. He didn't bother locking it. Sang Le hadn't taken a key with him.

Danny bounded down the stairs. Never had he felt so lighthearted and full of hope. His feet weren't going fast enough, so he started to jog. As he reached the end of the parking lot, where a large live oak tree spread its limbs, he heard a noise. He paused and glanced around. Maybe it was a cat. He started walking, then heard the noise again.

"Duong," a voice groaned.

Danny spun around and stared into the shadows around him. Then he saw something dark slumped over at the base of the oak tree. Danny rushed over and knelt down beside the boy propped against the tree trunk.

"Sang Le! What happened?"

"It is nothing," Sang Le said, his voice only a whisper. "Please take me inside. I will be all right if I rest a while."

"I'm going to call 911. Wait here."

"No, please." Sang Le grabbed Danny's shirt. His hands were covered with blood.

"You're bleeding! Come on, man, you're really hurt."

"No, please, take me inside. Don't tell anyone. Don't tell Bà. She will think I was with Cobra again. I will be all right after some rest." He struggled to rise to his feet, and Danny wrapped his arms around his cousin's shoulders. As they staggered a few feet, light from the street lamp fell across Sang Le's face. It was a lopsided mass of cuts, bruises, lumps, and blood.

"Oh, man, I don't believe this," Danny said, his voice shaking out of control. "I'm calling 911 right now. You're too bad to walk up those stairs." He gently lay Sang Le at the base of the tree again, but his cousin grabbed Danny's hand.

"Danny, you must tell Bà I kept my word," he said in a strained whisper. "I didn't go back to Cobra. Tell her, tell them all, I love them. I'm sorry I brought so much heartache. Tell Hong, my beautiful rose . . ." He paused and swallowed hard as a wave of pain swept over his face. "My beautiful rose, tell her . . ."

"I will, Sang Le," Danny said, surprised that tears were pooling in his eyes. "I'll tell her."

"The bad *ma qui*—my shadow spirits," Sang Le said softly, "they are gone at last. No more bad luck . . . no more . . ." Danny felt his cousin's grip tighten, then slowly loosen.

His neighbor, Mr. Tran, who was coming off the late shift, saw them and hurried over.

"Call 911!" Danny shouted. The man nodded and ran inside. Danny held his cousin in his arms. He rambled on and on about how everything was going to be all right, but Sang Le never opened his eyes or spoke. When the ambulance arrived, neighbors peeked out their windows. Danny watched the medics hover over Sang Le for a moment, then lift him onto the stretcher. One of them placed his hand on Danny's shoulder.

"Are you his relative?"

Danny nodded. "He's my cousin."

"Where are his parents?"

"They're dead. He lives with me. Is he going to be all right?"

"No, I'm afraid not. Your cousin is dead."

Chapter Fifteen

Danny's knees buckled and he grabbed the tree for support. He stared at the spot where his cousin had lain and saw a brown paper sack. In it were a pack of cigarettes and a small bag of popcorn. Absentmindedly, Danny picked the sack up and twisted it in his hands. Mr. Tran put his arm around Danny and tried to lead him away, but Danny shrugged off the man's hand.

"He can't be dead," Danny said at last. "Try again."

The medic shook his head. "Where are your parents, son? We need to talk to them right away."

Danny looked up at the large concrete breezeway that served as their patio. He saw Lan and Kim and Bà and his parents, all in their nightclothes. Bà's long hair was flowing down to her knees, making her look more like a child than an old woman. Danny closed his eyes. How could he tell her that her favorite grandchild, her hope, her love, was gone—senselessly beaten to death?

"Danny," Lan called out and rushed down the stairs. "You have a telephone call. It's Tiffany Schultz."

Danny scooped Lan into his arms to prevent her from getting close to the stretcher. He buried his face in her hair a moment.

"What's wrong, Danny? What happened? Why are the police here? Who's in the ambulance?"

Danny carried Lan up the stairs. He spoke to his father and mother softly, explaining what had happened. He was in the apartment when Bà began wailing. He closed his bedroom door and picked up the phone.

"Hello," he said in a voice so hoarse he didn't recognize it.

"Danny? Sorry to call you so late. Did I wake you up?" Her voice sounded nervous, like the first time they had dated.

"No." Danny sniffed and ran his shirt sleeve across his nose.

"I'm spending the night at Julie Martin's."

"Yeah, I know." Danny spoke methodically, hardly knowing what he was saying and amazed that his mouth could speak so calmly while his heart was throbbing with anguish. "I called your house earlier and Bradley told me. He said he was alone. You'd better call home and find out if he's okay."

"Thanks, Danny. I called a minute ago. Frank is back home now. Bradley's all right."

"Good. Tiffany—" He wanted to tell her that he couldn't talk now but she interrupted.

"Danny, a lot of stuff has happened this past week. I've been thinking. Maybe, well . . . maybe we should try one more time. I miss you so much. I really do love you." She paused. "Danny, are you crying?"

"Tiffany . . . I—I can't talk right now. There's been an accident. The police and ambulance are outside right now."

"Oh, no. What happened?"

"My cousin Sang Le. He's dead." Danny almost choked on the words. He fought to control his shaking voice.

"Dead. But . . . I just saw him about an hour ago."

Danny bolted up from the bed. "Where?"

"At Tilson's Grocery Store. Julie and Susan and I got hungry for ice cream and popcorn. I was sitting in the car when I saw Sang Le coming out of the store. He stopped and talked to me for a couple of minutes."

"What did he say?"

"That's why I called you. He told me you were depressed and miserable, and he was worried that you might do something desperate if I didn't call you." Her trembling voice suddenly cracked. "Oh, poor Sang Le. He was so sweet. I can't believe it."

"Did you see him talking to anyone else?"

A long silence hung in the air before she replied. "Is it important?"

"Someone beat my cousin to death."

Danny heard the gasp on the other end of the phone. For a few seconds he thought Tiffany was not going to answer. When she spoke her voice was small, like a scared little girl's.

"It can't be true. It just can't be."

"Tiffany, did you see anybody suspicious? Did you see some Vietnamese guys wearing black jackets with yellow cobras on the back?"

"I saw him talking to some guys," Tiffany said. "But I didn't know they would do anything to him. I can't believe they beat him to death. I just can't believe it. Oh, Danny, I'm so sorry."

"Did you recognize any of the guys? Was it Cobra?"

"I—I don't know who Cobra is. Danny, I've got to go now."

"No, wait. You've got to tell me what they looked like."

"I can't," she sobbed.

"Tiffany, wait—" A thud rang in Danny's ear as the receiver hit a tabletop. He could hear Tiffany crying hysterically and some other girl trying to comfort her. He shouted into the phone again and again. Finally someone picked up the receiver.

"Hello?" a girl said.

"Julie, this is Danny Vo. What's happening there? Let me speak to Tiffany again."

"She can't talk to you, Danny. She's too upset. I'm sorry about your cousin."

"Julie, did you and Susan get a good look at the guys who were talking to my cousin? Were they wearing black leather jackets with yellow cobras on the back? It's really important. I have to know."

"Susan and I were inside the store. We saw a Vietnamese boy leaving, but we didn't pay any attention. We didn't notice him talking to Tiffany and we didn't notice anybody talking to him. We didn't even know he was your cousin. I'm so sorry, Danny. I've gotta go now. We're taking Tiffany home. She's really losing it."

After Danny hung up the phone, he returned to the living room. Bà's shrieks had turned into soft whimpers. Everyone was gathered around her, and Danny hoped to slip out unnoticed. But her watery eyes pinned him as he walked by her chair.

"Grandson, you know who did this to my precious Sang Le," she said. "You must tell the police who did it."

"I don't know, Bà. I swear I don't."

"You knew him better than anyone else. Search your heart and you will know." Danny expected her to mention Cobra, but the words *toan du dang* never left her lips.

Outside, Danny approached the tall black officer who had taken charge. He rapidly scribbled notes in his notepad as he questioned everyone nearby. He wasn't very happy. No one had seen anything. One woman claimed she had heard some cries but thought it was the neighbor's cats fighting again.

The policeman put one foot on the bottom stair rung.

"You're the boy's cousin?" he asked.

"Yes, sir."

"Do you have any idea who might have done this? Was he mixed up in drugs or anything like that?"

"I never saw my cousin do drugs. I don't think this had anything to do with drugs."

"Any enemies?"

A picture of Cobra's hard black eyes flashed across Danny's mind. He shrugged. "I don't know."

The policeman frowned, then flipped his notepad closed.

"Now, why do I have the feeling that you're holding something back? If you know anything, you have to tell me. Are you trying to protect someone?"

"No!" Danny hated the way his voice squealed. "I want the murderer caught and punished. Believe me, I want it more than anything."

"All right." The officer reached into his shirt pocket and removed a business card. "If you or anyone else finds out anything new, give me a call. You know, being kicked and hit by a baseball bat is a terrible way to die."

"Kicked? Baseball bat? Are you sure?"

"Yes. The coroner saw boot imprints on his back and marks consistent with those made by a baseball bat. *Now* do you remember something I should know?"

Danny blinked over and over and tried to swallow down the sharp lump in his throat. He shook his head. Before the policeman could ask another question, Danny spun on his heels and began running toward Julie Martin's house as fast as his legs would carry him.

As he crossed the bayou bridge near her house, he saw Julie's car pulling out of the driveway. With a burst of speed, Danny charged in front of the car. Julie slammed on the brakes and rolled down her window.

"Danny? What—"

"Tiffany, get out!" he said between gasps for air. He jerked the passenger door open.

Tiffany's red, swollen eyes searched Danny's angry face. She didn't move. Danny grabbed her arm and pulled her out. Susan and Julie began screaming at him, but he didn't care.

"It was Frank, wasn't it?" he shouted into her pale face. "You saw your brother and his creepy friends talking to my cousin. That's why you're so upset, isn't it? You're worried that your brother may be arrested for murder." He shook her until tears started flowing from her blue eyes again.

"I know Frank didn't do it," she said in a trembling voice. "He couldn't have. It was Brian. Brian is the one who likes to hurt people. Frank couldn't kill anyone."

"Even if he didn't do the actual killing, he stood by and watched. He didn't stop it. He's just as guilty as Brian."

"Danny, please try to understand. Ever since our dad left, Frank's been so confused. He's all mixed up in the head right now, but he's not a murderer. I have to go home and talk to him and find out what happened."

"No, you have to go to the police and tell them what you saw."

"No, not yet. I have to talk to Frank and get his side of the story. I know he's innocent. I can't turn in my own brother."

"Then I will."

"Please, Danny." Tiffany's fingers dug into Danny's arm. "If you care about me at all, if you care about our future, please, please don't turn my brother in yet. Wait until I've talked to him. I love you more than anything, Danny. Please, don't ruin everything for us."

Danny felt as if someone had knocked the wind from his lungs. How many hundreds of nights had he laid awake tossing and turning, dreaming of the day Tiffany would say those words. He felt a rush of emotion as a layer of moisture formed on his eyes. He blinked to bring Tiffany's pale face into focus.

"I'm not the one who ruined everything," he said in a hoarse voice. "Your brother took care of that. He's the one who should pay for his crime, not me and not you. I saw what your brother was and his friend Brian, but I was blinded by love. All I cared about was you. And now my cousin is dead. He only talked to you to try to patch things up between us. He was just doing me a favor. He didn't deserve to die like that."

Tiffany jerked her hand away from Danny's arm.

"All right," she said in a raspy voice. "If you tell the police, I'll deny I ever saw my brother talking to Sang Le. It's just your word against mine."

Danny looked into the desperate eyes that he thought he knew so well, the eyes that he dreamed of every night.

"Do what you have to, Tiffany," he said slowly and released her arm. An overwhelming wave of depression swept over him as he watched her climb back into the car. The last thing he saw was her sad eyes looking at him through the rear window of the vanishing car.

As Danny walked back toward his apartment, his mind swirled with memories of Tiffany Marie. From the first time he had seen her to their first kiss to the time he held her in his arms and danced to slow music, his heart recalled everything. In the past three years, never once had he felt anything but love and desire. He knew she wasn't prejudiced like her brother; she was decent and good. They could have overcome their problems. She was ready to come back to him. They had a future together. If he remained quiet about Frank Schultz, she would be dedicated to Danny for life. If he turned Frank Schultz in, she would hate him forever.

Soon Danny was drowning in so many memories of Tiffany that he could not breathe. He stopped beside the bayou and watched the streetlights reflecting on the dark water below. What would it hurt if he didn't turn in Frank Schultz right away? He could just sit back and wait a day or two. He knew Tiffany would probably call the police sooner or later. She couldn't live with something like that on her conscience. But suppose his hesitation gave Frank and Brian and the others the chance to run away? They might never be caught and punished.

Danny squeezed his eyes closed and tried to imagine Tiffany's beautiful face, but all he saw was the pain in Sang Le's eyes as he lay dying under the oak tree. Even as he died, he only cared about the feelings of others—Bà, his aunt and uncle, Hong. His whole life had been one sacrifice after another for the happiness of others.

Danny looked at the water and the tall, waving spring grass. It reminded him of something long ago and far away. He breathed in air filled with the tangy fragrance of wild weeds and the warmth of damp earth. The River of Perfumes had smelled like that the day he fell into the lotus-filled moat. Sang Le had risked his life and lost everything to save Danny that day, yet he never blamed his little cousin for his unfortunate life. Even as he died, Sang Le did not blame Danny.

From his pants pocket, Danny removed the small black velvet box that held Tiffany's ring. He should have returned it to the jeweler and gotten a refund instead of a different size. But now it was too late. With a scream, he hurled it across the bank and watched the black waters swallow it. He stood there as the concentric circles radiated out, then slowly faded, and the dark water grew still again.

When Danny arrived at the apartment, the police officer was standing in front of Bà's favorite chair. His huge form almost hid the old woman's frail body.

All eyes turned toward Danny as he entered the door, but it was Bà's glowing black eyes that Danny saw as he stepped toward her.

"Did you remember something, son?" the policeman asked.

Danny kneeled in front of Bà and took her withered hands into his. He nodded to the policeman.

"Yes," he said, as he looked into the ancient black eyes. "I did remember something, sir. I remembered that the blood of a dragon flows through my veins. Just as it flowed through my cousin's veins. An honorable, brave dragon that will do anything for his family, no matter what the cost. Yes, I did remember something after all, officer. I remembered who I am."

The policeman looked puzzled, but Bà nodded, then pulled her grandson close and hugged him with all her might.

Epilogue

Danny hammered the last nail through the metal tray girdled around the oak tree where Sang Le had died. The first one he had built had been knocked down the night before by a neighborhood dog trying to get to the food offerings. He built the new one higher, four feet off the ground. Bà, wearing a white headband to signify she was still in mourning, stood on her tiptoes as she carefully placed on the altar a photograph of Sang Le, a bowl of rice, flowers, and a bitter melon from the vine that now rambled over the roof of their apartment. She lit three joss sticks, prayed silently, then touched them three times to her forehead before bowing and placing them on the tray. The sweet fragrance of sandalwood drifted into the humid summer air. Above them, dark clouds churned and thunder rumbled.

Kim walked by carrying a box of shoes and toys. She handed them to her father who was standing beside a U-Haul trailer hooked to his car. Uncle Dao climbed down the stairs holding the family's vacuum cleaner, and close behind him came Thuy carrying a bag of trash. Aunt Lien and Lan walked cautiously with armloads of clothes.

"That's the last of everything," Danny's mother shouted from the landing. She held a broom in one hand and a dust bin in the other. "I will be finished here in a few minutes."

Mr. Vo leapt down from the trailer and walked over to Bà. "Mother," he said softly in Vietnamese. "It is time to go. Our new house is waiting. We must hurry before it starts to rain."

Bà nodded.

"Thank you for repairing the altar, grandson," she said to Danny. "Sang Le's spirit will appreciate it, I'm sure. I do not want to leave this place. Who will take care of his *am* after we move away?"

"You can still come to visit. Our new house is only a couple of blocks away. It's time to go now." He let the old woman bow three times again and pray silently a few seconds before leading her by the elbow to his father's car, where his parents were waiting.

As Danny slid into the driver's seat of his mother's car, next to his brother and sisters, he noticed Kim staring at something in the parking lot.

"Danny?" she whispered. "Who's that?"

Danny turned around. His heart stopped, then started to race. Slowly he got out and walked closer.

"Tiffany? What are you doing here?" Even without makeup she was still beautiful, but her face was not as full of life as he had remembered. She seemed older than the last time he had seen her three months ago, and thinner.

"I just came to say good-bye." She bit her lip and her blue eyes searched his face.

Danny drew in his breath and let it out slowly. He wanted to force a smile and tell her everything was okay, no hard feelings, but he couldn't. He had spent too many restless nights worrying about what Tiffany thought of him for turning in her brother and his skinhead friends. She had not called him once, nor responded to his letters. She had dropped out of school and out of his life. At a time when she most needed a friend, she turned away from everyone and built a wall around herself.

Danny cleared his throat and jammed his hands into his shorts pockets.

"Okay. Good-bye, Tiffany."

She glanced at the U-Haul slowly pulling out of the parking lot. "I heard you were moving."

He nodded. "The newspaper started a memorial fund in Sang Le's name. The Vietnamese community contributed so much it was unbelievable. We gave the extra money to a Hong Kong refugee camp charity. When someone read that it was my cousin's biggest dream that his grandmother move into a house, he donated a house to us with no down payment."

"We moved, too," Tiffany said in a soft, almost timid voice. "My mom sold our house to pay for Frank's lawyer fees and bail. We live in an apartment on the other side of town now. I hate going to a different school, but I guess it's just as well."

Danny shifted his weight. He didn't know if he should feel sorry for her or not. Part of him wanted to say "You got what you deserved for defending your brother," but another part of him wanted to tell her he understood what she was going through—the newspapers, the TV stations, the police, the neighbors, and disrupted family life.

"Well, I just wanted to say good-bye. And, and . . ." She stared at the ground. Danny saw two large teardrops rolling down her smooth cheeks. Suddenly she jerked her head up and looked him squarely in the eyes.

"Danny, please don't hate me."

Danny swallowed hard and fought to keep the emotion from his voice. "Why should I hate you, Tiffany?"

She closed her eyes and slowly exhaled. A dark cloud seemed to lift from her face.

"For what my brother did. I'm sorry I didn't try to stop him and Brian when I saw them talking to your cousin. You have to believe me."

Danny hesitated a moment. He didn't want to get into an argument with Tiffany, but so many questions had been left unanswered about that night. Suddenly he couldn't hold back. "That's something I don't get, Tiffany. Why didn't you go inside the store and tell Mr. Tilson, or call the police? You knew those skinheads hated Vietnamese people. Why didn't you do something?"

"Don't you think I know all that? I don't sleep anymore for thinking how maybe I could have stopped them. But I swear I didn't know my own brother would do something like that. You've got to believe me, Danny. I didn't know they would kill your cousin."

A wave of pity suddenly swept over Danny as Tiffany broke into sobs. He wanted to pull her close. His arms ached to hold her as he watched the tears spilling down her face and her body softly trembling, but he could not move. After a few minutes, she pulled a crumpled tissue from her pocket and blew her nose.

"Frank's trial is next month," she said. "He's eighteen. They're trying him as an adult. He may go to prison for the rest of his life."

"That's too bad." Danny held his tongue in check to keep from blurting out his real feelings about Frank Schultz. There was no point in making Tiffany more upset.

"It was Brian who used the baseball bat," she said. "Frank says he tried to stop Brian when he saw how bad your cousin was getting hurt, but Brian went crazy."

"Well, I guess Brian won't be telling anybody his side of the story, will he?"

"You know who murdered Brian, don't you?"

Danny shrugged. A memory flashed through his head—the look of pain and hatred in Cobra's eyes the day of Sang Le's funeral, and Danny at the cemetery pleading with the ponytailed gang leader not to do anything desperate, especially to Frank Schultz. Ironic, he thought, that Tiffany's brother was still alive only because Cobra respected Sang Le and honored his cousin's plea.

"My brother knows he was wrong," Tiffany continued. "He's really, really sorry about what happened. It's changed him. He's not a mean person, Danny; he just got all messed up because our dad left. Mom tried to raise him right, but, well, you know how it is when a guy joins a gang, he only listens to the leader. Frank had a lot of bad luck; everything he tried seemed to go wrong."

"Maybe he had bad spirits living in his shadow."

"What?"

"Nothing."

"My mother is a wreck because of everything. I have to take care of Bradley all the time now. The lawyer said I shouldn't talk to anyone before the trial, especially you, but I just had to say good-bye. I guess I'll never see you again."

"Then I guess it's good-bye forever," he replied. Danny's heart pounded as Tiffany took a step closer. She hesitated a moment, as if hoping for a change of heart.

"I'll always love you, Danny Vo," she said softly and quickly kissed his cheek. She turned and ran toward the red Mustang parked along the street curb.

Danny fought the fury that raged in his heart. If Tiffany had stood up to her brother or told the store clerk to call the police, maybe Sang Le would be alive today. In a way she was partly responsible for his death. She would probably tell the jury that her brother was a sweet guy, just mixed up with a bad crowd.

Danny wanted to hate her. He wanted to shout at the vanishing Mustang that he was glad he would never see her again. But his heart thundered in his chest and each beat ached with pain at the thought of never hearing her voice or seeing her face or touching her hand again.

"I'll always love you, too, Tiffany Marie Schultz," he whispered to the churning sky.

Danny didn't know if he would ever see her again. Even if he did, he didn't know if it would be possible for his family to accept her, or for her family to accept him. Maybe they would meet again someday, start all over, and marry. Or maybe Danny would end up marrying an old-fashioned girl like Hong. She had been extremely kind and supportive and strong after Sang Le's death, and Danny had leaned on her more than he thought possible.

As Danny returned to the car, the sun suddenly burst through the clouds for a fleeting second. The black shadow of the oak tree fell across his face. Danny looked at the altar where the incense was still smoldering. He thought about Sang Le, who had made so many heroic sacrifices and done so many honorable, good things, and yet had gotten mixed up with an evil force like Cobra. Sang Le believed that everyone has good and bad in them, that all your evil spirits live in your shadow. Maybe he was right. Maybe Sang Le was just as bad as Frank Schultz or maybe Frank was just as good as Sang Le. Maybe you can't kill the bad shadow spirits without killing yourself. Maybe the only hope is to keep those bad spirits in your shadow where they belong.

As Danny started the car, rain began to dance on the hood. He wondered if he would ever be able to think of Sang Le without thinking of Tiffany or Frank or Cobra or Hong. They were like plants growing too close together in the same pot, whose roots get all tangled up. Not one of them could be pulled up without damaging them all. In his heart Danny knew that Sang Le's death had hurt Tiffany and Hong and Cobra as much as it had hurt him and Bà.

Danny turned the car around in the parking lot and stared at the street that led to the waiting new house and new life. A gust of wind rocked the car and he turned the windshield wipers to high speed.

"Bà says the rain will bring us good luck in our new house," Lan said as she wiped the foggy window and watched rain drench the parched earth. "She says the clouds are the shadows of lucky dragons."

"That's just a superstition, isn't it, Danny?" Kim insisted.

"There really aren't such things as dragons, are there?" Thuy asked.

Three pairs of eager eyes turned to their older brother, awaiting his reply. Danny glanced at the altar around the oak tree, its incense snuffed out and its flowers beaten down by the cold, slanted rain. Maybe Sang Le had not lived in the lucky shadow of a dragon after all, or maybe lucky dragons didn't exist in America, but Danny knew his cousin had touched all of their lives and he would be a part of them forever. And Danny knew exactly how Sang Le would answer the children.

"Dragons? Of course, there are dragons. We all have the blood of a mighty dragon flowing through our veins. Hasn't Bà ever told you that story? No? Then I'll tell you now. Long, long ago, a handsome dragon-lord named Lac-Long-Quan met a beautiful princess named Au-Co on a misty mountain in Vietnam . . ."